GOD SMITES

and Other Muslim Girl Problems

GOD SMITES

and Other Muslim Girl Problems

An Asiya Haque Mystery

Ishara Deen

Deeya Publishing Inc.
www.deeyapublishing.com

Deeya Publishing Inc.

God Smites and Other Muslim Girl Problems
Copyright © 2017 by Ishara Deen

First Canadian edition January 2017

For more information about special discounts for bulk purchases contact Deeya Publishing Inc. at info@deeyapublishing.com

Library and Archives Canada Cataloguing in Publication information is available upon request

ISBN: 0-9958336-0-5 (print)
ISBN: 0-9958336-1-3 (ebook)
ISBN-13: 978-0-9958336-0-9 (print)
ISBN-13: 978-0-9958336-1-6 (ebook)

For all the girls who were never told someone like them could, not even in books.

1

Ma pressed the tip of her index finger against the kitchen table to stress the importance of what she was saying.

"When the man and the woman are alone together," her eyes, open big and wide, caught mine, "Satan is the third."

"Yes, Ma," I said in my most gentle, most obedient voice. I cleared my throat. "Abbu's waiting in the car. I should…"

"The only way to be protected is to stay away from the boys." Ma continued.

By boys, Ma meant the male gender in its entirety. Which would be a little difficult considering about half the people where I volunteered, including my pain-in-the-butt boss, were male. "Yes, Ma. You told me last week."

And the week before, and the week before that, and every week since I started at the Sheriden Conservation Centre to collect my 40 volunteer hours in order to graduate high school.

"Asiya, it is very important that you remember."

It's times like these I always remind myself of this story from Prophet Mohammed's life. So basically, this guy came up to the Prophet and for some random reason asked him who most deserved his best behaviour. The Prophet answered, "Your mother."

The guy didn't seem to like that answer much because he asked the same question again. The Prophet answered, "Your mother," again.

The man probably had a mom like mine because he asked a third time, "Then who?" and the Prophet replied again, "Your mother."

Dude, really didn't get the point because he tried again, "Then who?" The Prophet probably got tired by then or something, because he finally said, "Your father."

Whenever Imams talk about this incidence in the *masjid,* they say it's because moms go through so much pain during child birth, that we can never repay them, even for the pain of a single contraction. And then I'm reminded of health class and Mrs. Clavier's analogy for cervix dilation in labour: basically it starts the size of a Cheerio, expands through contractions to the size of a bagel, and then that's it. The watermelon of a baby somehow squeezes through the bagel-sized cervix. I remind myself of this obsessively often: I was a watermelon, Ma was a bagel, therefore I owe her big time.

With renewed patience, I told Ma, "I remember," just as I did every week before volunteering. And every week, she took extra time to make sure I got the point: me + boy = invitation for Satan. I just wished this conversation didn't make me perpetually late.

I snuck a quick glance to the microwave for the time.

Ma caught it. Her lips tightened and her nostrils flared. "You did not remember when you jumped on that boy!"

"Ma!" I stopped myself from rolling my eyes. "I've been telling you since Grade 4, he took my Dunkaroos!"

"You should never jump on boys. For any reason."

"I haven't since!"

"You let them touch your legs!"

"With their feet when they took cheap shots while we played soccer!" I huffed, more angry at myself than anyone else for getting baited into an argument I couldn't win. I sucked in a slow breath, and reminded myself: *watermelon/ bagel, watermelon/bagel.* With my impatience contained, I tried again. "I haven't played soccer or anything with boys since junior high, okay?"

Ma's eyes scrutinized me, as if she could see residual signs of sluttiness on my face. Which in Ma's world included conversations with, or even physical proximity to, boys.

I flipped my braid over my shoulder and undid the tie, dragging my fingers through the mess of black curls over and over. I'd been good at soccer and really good at track, but I gave them both up since school teams require staying after school, which – surprise – is a fat no in Ma's book. And since pretty much everyone stopped thinking the opposite sex had cooties in middle school, I gave up having a steady group of friends. I pulled straight A's. I helped Adil, my younger brother, with his homework. I did what I could to help around the house. So I had been an exceptionally big watermelon, I did not deserve this.

I took a deep breath as I finished retying my freshly braided hair. I looked Ma in the eyes. "No jumping, no sports, no letting guys touch my legs, no being alone with boys, period. I haven't done any of it, I promise."

Out of nowhere Michael's sombre eyes and shy smile, flashed in my mind. I shoved the thought back, way back. I had nothing to feel guilty about. I mean okay, I thought he was good looking, but most people would. And so he stopped by to talk to Em and me at lunch… every day. It was just polite conversation.

Although lately, it did seem Em was right. He did talk to me more than her. But we had English class together, so it made sense we'd have more to talk about. And it wasn't like I was alone with him. And I wasn't planning to be. When would I be? I never had the chance. Not that I would if I did…I mean…oh shoot. My gaze refocused on Ma.

From the distant frown-pout on her face, she'd been busy with her own thoughts. "I do not like you going to this volunteering so near to the jungle."

It was more like a wood that lined the edge of Sheriden, the suburb of a suburb we lived in, but I said, "I know, Ma."

"You should have volunteered at the masjid where you would have been safe."

Where I would have been cooking with the other women for the weekly soup kitchen they held. No offense to the homeless, but I needed other skills if I ever wanted a job. I didn't know what I wanted to do, but I knew it wasn't being a chef, and it definitely wasn't being a housewife.

Thank you, God, for at least letting Abbu agree with me on that.

"It's too late to change that now." I tried to look appropriately sad even as a little thump pulsed in my chest. *I'm sorry God, please forgive me for...* Okay, maybe asking God's forgiveness was a little much considering I'd be drawing this lie out for the rest of the school year. I decided to go with, *God, have mercy. Please don't smite me for lying to my mother.* "I have to finish there if I want to graduate and go to university."

And there it was, the magic key that made the biggest sacrifices okay in our family: higher education.

"*Atcha*, fine." Ma heaved a sigh. "You are keeping your Abbu waiting. Go."

2

"Vicki!" I hissed. I spotted the auburn hair she always wrapped into a beehive the second I tiptoed into the front hall. "Where is he?"

"Commander Green?" She tapped her pursed lips, pretending to think. "Probably in his office contemplating whether to cross the line over to ecoterrorism when he should be working on getting us a gazebo. Do you know how many people would come out here for weddings if we had a gazebo?"

Vicky and Nate always butted heads. She thought the Centre should focus on building people-friendly ways to get into nature. He thought we were at war.

"What kind of mood is he in?" I asked. Even though Vicky was the assistant manager, we all worked together to survive Nate.

Vicky tapped her lips. "I'd say he's more of a pain in the ass than usual." She checked her watch. "He won't be happy you're late again."

I knew that.

"Was he calm after his walk?" Nate was at his best in nature. He walked the woods before and after every shift at work. I think the solitary time helped him tolerate having to talk to us.

"He didn't go," Vicky said. "Barely made it in on time himself today,"

"Great." He'd be totally grumpy. I yanked off my jacket as I slipped into the office and crept toward my desk. Maybe if I dumped my jacket before he saw I could pretend like I'd been there the whole t–

"Asiya." Nate stepped out of his office, his exceptionally good posture making him look like a drill sergeant. Considering he'd spent over a decade voluntouring the world after his Environmental Science degree, I wondered where Nate got his rigidity. Despite being in his early forties, Nate looked like Drake – early baby-faced Drake with the cardigan obsession – so the drill sergeant thing was more annoying than scary. "You are late."

"I'm sorry." I turned to face him. "I–"

"We can converse further in my office." And he was gone, back into command central.

I dropped my jacket on my chair, gripping the padding on the back of the chair as I tried to calm down. He wouldn't fire me. I mean, I worked for free. Who got fired from volunteering?

Please God, don't let it be me.

I slinked into Nate's uber-organized, minimalist office,

where as usual his desk was completely empty except for his laptop, reusable water bottle, and a globe. I knew from past visits that each time he left the office, he moved the globe back between the two metal fists on his shelf where his bike helmet currently rested.

I pulled back one of the two chairs across his desk and sat. "Nate, I–"

Seeing his scowl, I shuffled forward until the chairs were once again inline.

Nate nodded his approval before starting. "It's been a few consecutive weeks of this and today, I don't have the patience to tolerate it."

"I'm really sorry I'm late, I–"

"Let's skip the excuses."

My mouth clamped shut.

"Let's just get it out there, okay? I know you're not late because you're the second last one in your carpool."

Oh.

"And I know your carpool consists of you and your father."

Uh-oh.

"And I know your father's car has horrible fuel efficiency."

Dammit, I hadn't even thought of that one.

"And I know that's been the case since day one."

Since this was going nowhere, I figured I might as well ask. "Am I that bad a liar?"

"Yes," Nate said. "But also, your mom calls me. Every week while you're on your way over here to remind me of the rules where you're concerned."

"Oh."

"For example, according to her, you should have left the door open since you're alone with me – a man – but I figured if you didn't want me to know the deal bad enough to lie, you didn't want the whole office to know either."

I swallowed. On some level, I recognized that Nate was being really nice about this, but mostly I was focused on how humiliating it was. It was one thing for me to have to tolerate Ma's lectures, but it was too much to expect Nate to do it too.

"I understand having an embarrassing mother, believe me, I do," Nate said. "But I can't deal with this every week."

"Okay." My chest hurt and my arms felt numb. I nodded and stood. "I get it."

"If I'm going to have to take calls from your mother each week, I can't be spending time doing this dance with you when you get here too."

"You're letting me stay?"

"Uh, are corporate interests encroaching each day? Is urban sprawl attacking?" Nate stood. "Are people so greedy for property they'll cut down the woods and with it the very air we breathe to get it?"

Commander Green was back. Somehow Nate's intensity didn't bother me as much anymore.

"Your work on Facebook and Twitter is engaging a totally different demographic than we usually get," Nate said. "I can't afford to let you go."

I felt a little glow. It was a tiny thing, but still, it was nice to feel competent at something other than school.

"I'd like to start Instagram and Snapchat accounts too," I said. "The woods are still summer green and I thought it would be really nice if we posted pictures regularly, then pulled them all together into this time-lapsed video that shows how beautiful the woods are in every season."

"Excellent," Nate said. "Go take them." He paused, the possibility of a smile on his lips. "Just don't tell your mother I said that."

Still a little embarrassed, I decided to grab my jacket and go out to take pictures right away. I felt a little nudge of guilt like I did every time I went walking in the woods during break. I tried my best not to do things my parents didn't approve of, but time to myself somewhere as peaceful as the woods was too hard to pass up.

I hoofed it to where the hiking trail started, taking in deep breaths of fresh woods air on the way. The creek burbled in the distance. A slow breeze rustled the leaves overhead and the sound of creatures scampering through the trees met me. Abbu loved being in nature like I did. He said it reminded him of the majesty of Allah. Ma thought it was full of things to be feared. Any place I wasn't strictly chaperoned was.

I kicked a stone on the trail. I'd be graduating soon. If it were up to Ma, Abbu would drive me to and from the nearest university until I graduated. After which, Nasreen Aunty would find the boringest Bengali guy she could for me to marry, just like my older sister, Afiya, had. Without ever having lived.

Everyone in my grade was making plans for distant schools, first steps toward careers, and travel far from here. They were ready for the general beginning of their grown-up lives, and I didn't know what living meant. *What do I want?*

"Asiya."

I froze. And then turned slowly, wondering if I was a witch. Because I was pretty sure I'd just conjured Michael.

3

I'd been wrong. The trees weren't summer green anymore. As I walked along the trail, I could see they'd lost enough chlorophyll to no longer be the colours of emeralds and shamrocks and moss. I snapped a few pictures, capturing the gold tones that shone through the leaves, making them closer to the colour of limes and pears and pistachios. I took picture after picture, focusing on my work because I didn't know what to do about Michael walking beside me.

When I saw Michael behind me at the edge of the woods a few minutes ago, I'd thought, *You're not really here.*

He'd laughed. And I realized I'd said it at the same time that I thought it. That was the dangerous thing about being with Michael. I didn't feel the need to watch myself and put on my usual reserve.

The first time I'd talked to Michael – was the beginning

of school only a few weeks ago? – I'd been cursing Em's ex-boyfriend, Bryant. I'd known there was a new kid, the school was buzzing about it. I'd taken one look at Michael from across the cafeteria: tall, square jawed, the I'm-too-cool-to-care-about-my-hair-and-clothes look, and knew without a doubt he'd end up hanging out with the popular kids. They scooped him up in seconds.

Em and I were not the popular kids. We were, for lack of a better word, and at the risk of sounding like sufficiently fibrous bowel movements, floaters. Not in any group, not unwelcome either. Basically, Em changed guys (and styles) with the seasons and since the moving on let me be friendly with everyone without actually being close to anyone, the setup worked well with my out-of-school social limitations.

What hadn't worked well was Em's summer fling with Bryant, since he was a rotting piece of arrogant turd who'd hurt my best friend. As a result, she was doing a guys-can-go-to-hell goth look this fall, which, as far as the new guy was concerned, pretty much meant I'd never talk to him. Except that one day at lunch, Em was down and I was in the middle of trying to cheer her up with optimistic possibilities like Bryant's genitals getting attacked by a slow-acting, flesh-eating disease, when a new voice joined into the conversation.

"Ouch." A quiet, but somehow solid male voice I'd never heard before, asked. "What did the bastard do to deserve that?"

Em didn't bother hiding it. "He cheated on me and when I broke up with him he sent around a picture of us where he drew an arrow pointing at my chest with the caption, 'Not much to move on from.'"

My eyes narrowed, watching Michael for any flicker down from Em's face, but he'd turned to shoot a disgusted glare across the cafeteria at Bryant. "He seems like that kind of guy."

"How do you know that?" I asked.

Michael blinked. When his deep-set eyes reopened, his irises, an unremarkable grey-blue a moment ago, sparked with thoughts and feelings and history. All of which I'd wanted to wade into. And then his lips formed a forced smile, wiping all emotion out of his eyes in the process. "I know the type."

Michael stayed with us for a few minutes, hearing out the other happy scenarios we'd come up with for Bryant. After that day, he still sat with the popular kids at first, but he'd make his rounds around the cafeteria, stopping by at some point or another to chat with Em and I. And when he did, it wasn't friendly, but far, like with everyone else at school. It was free, like the way I could be me when it was just me and Em. Except time moved a little faster when Michael was around. So, as he strolled the woods at my side, I tried to focus on picture-taking to slow down time and my runny mouth.

"You're quiet," Michael said.

Oh, that's because I'm waiting to see if being alone with you is going to result in a cataclysmic God smite. "Am I?"

I tried to relax, but I couldn't and I didn't know why.

It's just a walk.

It's just a walk.

It's just a walk with a guy I have a crush on alone in the woods.

It wasn't like I really believed Satan would appear at any second, commanding me beyond my will to do his bidding.

But then I figured that wasn't how Satan rolled. I wondered how Ma thought it worked. I mean, it wasn't like just cause Michael and I were alone together we were going to suddenly tear our clothes off like we'd caught some hormone-affecting virus that made us itch with a raging need to fornicate.

I turned to look at Michael. He gave me a reassuring smile from across the two feet I'd put between us. I threw a robotic smile across the distance, and added another half foot.

I mean, I didn't feel itchy, did I? No. I didn't. And if I did, it was because mosquitoes got me. Damn mosquitoes. It was not because I wanted to have sex with Michael. Although theoretically, if I did want to have sex, Michael was a good looking choice. Not that it was all about looks… was it? I mean technically, could you like someone and not be physically attracted to them? Em had sex with a complete asshole, but then she was an absolute romantic who wanted to see what wasn't there. Other than Em, I mostly knew what I watched on TV and it was pretty much the other way around: no need to like someone. As long as they were physically attractive, you were good to go. Michael probably knew, I mean there was no way a guy like him had never had sex. Whoa, I was walking beside a guy who'd probably had his penis *in somebody*. Some girl I didn't want to think about. Eww. Scratch her out. Even without her, it was still pretty unbelievable. Michael was capable of feeling something so strongly that enough blood flowed to his penis to make it hard like…

"What are you thinking about?"

"Wood. The woods. I really like the woods," I said, wishing for once my crazy curls were down so I could hide behind their massiveness.

"Yeah," Michael said, his eyes narrowing, like he was going to challenge my answer. But then his eyes dropped to the trail in front of us. "Would you rather I not be here?"

"No. I mean yes. I mean, I'm happy to see you," I said, unable to lie to him. "I'm just surprised. How did you know where to find me?"

"Don't get mad." Michael prefaced.

"Em?"

He nodded. "She said you take a walk during break and it was my best chance of catching you."

He wanted to catch me.

Ugh. First Ma put viral Satanic sex infections in my head, and now Em had me vomiting rom-com drivel. I loved that girl like she was my sister instead of the fake, catty beast of an older sibling I actually had, but I was going to kill her for this.

"This is an awesome trail for jogging," Michael said.

Before I could tell him I'd thought the exact same thing, Michael added. "We should run together some time."

Was he... with my pulse picking up, I had to work to sound calm. "How do you know I run?"

"The first time I saw you, you were racing Catrina at lunch. Em was screaming her head off, like you were about to take the gold in the Olympics, so I figured I might as well watch."

"Em's the best," I said, thinking killing her was overly harsh. Maybe I'd just maim her.

"From what I can tell, you're the best," Michael said. "I don't get why Catrina leads our track team if you're faster. You've got better form so I wouldn't be surprised if you run long distance too."

I knew he was talking about my running stance, but I felt myself getting warm at the idea of his eyes on my body.

"I can't do track," I said. "My…" I didn't want to have to tell Michael how weird my family was. For once, I wanted to just be here and hang out, like a normal person.

"I'll tell you what," Michael said. "You tell me what you were just going to say, and I'll tell you a secret about me."

"A secret?" I raised a doubtful eyebrow. "How do I know it's any good?"

Michael returned an arched brow, his mocking. "It's so good, no one else at our school knows."

Damn him, he had me. "Fine." I shoved the words out as quickly as possible. "My family is Muslim, the strict kind. I don't run track, or play soccer, or go jogging with guy friends because I'm not allowed."

"No jogging with guy friends?" He asked.

"No guy friends." I'd meant to say it firmly but my voice might have held a tinge of regret.

"Okay," Michael said, sounding not like it was okay, but like he was processing.

I waited for the barrage of questions on my weird reality when Michael levelled me with the words, "I came to Sheriden to find my parents."

What did he mean *find them*? "I thought you came here with them."

"Yeah, the official story at school is I moved here to be near family," Michael said. "People just assume I did it with my parents."

"So, do you have adoptive parents?"

"No."

That single word was so heavy and solitary that it hurt to hear it.

Michael stared straight ahead. "I aged out of the foster system."

"That means, you're…"

"Eighteen." Michael flicked a glance at me before dropping his gaze to the ground. "I, um, got into a bit of trouble and got behind in school."

I was still stuck on the fact that he didn't have a family. As much as mine suffocated me, I didn't know what I'd do without them. I spoke softly to smooth over the hurt I hadn't meant to cause. "I was going to say, that means you're here on your own."

"Oh. Yeah."

I still couldn't cross the street without someone holding my hand, and Michael *lived on his own*. Wow, we had *so* much in common. Even if I were willing to sneak around to see him, this thing with him wouldn't work out just because of my sheer boringness.

I shook my head. "I don't get what you're doing here with me."

"I was looking for a running buddy," Michael said, sadness falling away and a hint of a smile touched his voice. "But since that's out, I'm thinking I could use some help sharpening up my curses. Flesh-eating genital disease is pretty creative."

I laughed despite myself. "That's what you're into? You like girls who can run and curse."

My eyes popped open and I physically cringed. *Oh my God, I'd just assumed he was into me. Out loud.* "I mean… I wasn't trying to…"

Michael stopped me with a touch of his fingers to my arm. "I do like you when you run and when you curse. I also like how your mind connects things I would never think of. And I like it even better when you connect things in your head that make you blush and make me wonder what I could do to get you to tell me." He took my hand in his, his thumb swiping over my knuckles. "Like right now. What are you thinking, Asiya?"

Thinking? I wasn't thinking. His words and fingers and thumb were causing a wave of emotions to hit me like a belly flop. An all over, face-to-feet body smack. He was only holding my hand but the point of contact seemed like a beacon of sensation that flowed up my arm to warm my entire body. And from that same point of contact, an insistent pulse sounded off. An alarm system warning that wouldn't shut down until I acknowledged there was an intruder.

"I'm sorry." I pulled my hand from his. "I can't do this."

Michael's lips tightened a fraction but seeing my regret must have strengthened his resolve. "What if they met me?"

"My parents?" A surprised laugh burbled out of me. "They can never know about you."

"Even if I was really respectful of your culture rules?"

He really was adorable. "Just daring to be in the presence of their daughter would be a colossal sign of disrespect."

"Oh," Michael said.

"Yeah," I said, sad that he finally got it.

"Your parents say no… and that's what you want too?"

Or not.

"If I could have a guy for a friend, I would want it to be you," I said, unable to quite meet his eyes. "I know I'm supposed to be all about teenage rebellion and that this is thoroughly uncool, but… I don't want to let them down."

"I don't care about cool." Michael's eyes softened. "You're loyal." He didn't say it like he thought I was stupid for being devoted to people who restricted me. He said it like he wanted some of it for himself.

I didn't want our walk to end, but dragging this on was only making things harder. I sighed. "I should get back."

Michael nodded, and we turned back on the trail. A heavy silence hovered over us, making the calm peace of the woods seem dreary. I'd put an end to it. No more chances of catching non-existent sexual sicknesses. But if this was going to be the one and only time we'd hang out the two us, I didn't want it to end like this.

"So, about that run," I said, cutting a glance at Michael as I made sure my phone was properly tucked into my pocket. "I'll race you back!"

I took off before I finished speaking. I wasn't even sure I finished speaking because I was too busy running and laughing. My laughter died quickly when I realized my head start did nothing for me. After yelling I was a cheat, Michael was off. I could hear his heavier tread gaining on me immediately. Not only was he a runner, but he had over half a foot in height on me which meant a huge leg-span advantage. There was no way, I'd beat him on the trail.

I swerved a sharp right into the thicket, hoping to cut across the curve in the trail through the trees.

"Just wait until I catch you, you little cheat!" Michael abandoned the trail to follow behind me. I grinned. He'd have a harder time manoeuvering through the trees with his bigger frame.

"I didn't say 'on the trail.'" I shouted without turning.

When I didn't hear a response, I dared a quick turn to catch a glimpse of his position. "Don't assume you -whoa!"

I tripped. My foot caught on a log and sent me flying into the air and crashing down on my palms and knees.

"Asiya? Are you okay?" Michael's footsteps slowed as he approached.

"I'm okay." Other than feeling like an idiot. I turned onto my butt, holding in a groan from my bruised knees. "There was a fallen tree or something."

Michael didn't answer. He'd stopped a few feet away and was staring down at the log in disbelief.

I pushed myself up and went back to see what...

Michael wasn't looking at a log. And I hadn't fallen on a tree.

Nestled into the tall weeds lay a woman.

And she was dead.

4

I looked away immediately. But even after only a quick glance, I couldn't get her cold glassy eyes and bloodied head out from my inner eye.

Michael had no such problem. He stared. And stared with red eyes that looked like they might tear up.

He looked so upset that for a second I wondered if maybe… Could this woman be the birth mother he was looking for? Wait. I glanced back at her. Even bleached of colour, it was obvious from her features she was not fully white. And from what I could see, Michael was. It was possible Michael had gotten his features through recessive genes but, how likely was that? And why was I thinking about dominant and recessive gene traits right now? Probably because I wanted to think about anything other than the dead body three feet away. "Michael, what should we do?"

He didn't hear me. He was still staring at her, like he'd lost something.

"Michael." I went up to him and when he didn't respond again, I put my hand to his jaw and turned him to face me. "What are we going to do?"

Michael blinked at me like he was just remembering I was there. "Asiya. You have to go."

"We should call the police."

"I will," Michael said. He seemed to finally be back in his head and processing the situation. "But if we report it together your parents will know we were here together."

I sucked in a breath.

"I know," he said. "Just go."

"I don't want to leave you here alone."

"It's okay." Michael took my arm and guided me back to the trail. "I'll call the police and wait for them here."

It felt wrong to leave him to deal with this alone. I knew the right thing was to own up to what we'd found, where we were. Together. I was trembling with the need to do it.

"Come with me," I said, taking his hand and turning toward the Centre. "You can call the police from the Centre."

Michael dug in, pulling us to a stop. "I'd just have to come back to show them where she is, and it would be harder to find the exact spot."

Michael smoothed a loose curl behind my ear with a shaky hand. "I'll be okay. I promise."

I could see Michael was telling himself that as much as he was telling me. I could tell he was scared just like I was. "I should—"

"Just go already!" Michael burst out.

I stumbled back, blinking in surprise. The veins in Michael's face were tight like he was about to hulk out, or cry.

"I'm sorry."

In an instant, all that heat and anger was gone. Michael's red eyes weighed heavy with regret. "It's just that I should wait until you're back until I call. So no one suspects you were here. And the longer you take to go, the longer I have to stay out here."

"You're right," I said. It felt completely wrong, but Michael was giving me the option to save my butt and get far away from here. So I took it. I ran.

I headed back wondering how I would sit there pretending I hadn't just looked into the face of a woman with the life missing from her eyes. Just as I was almost out of view, I glanced back. It must have been the tears threatening my eyes confusing me, because I thought I saw Michael turn back toward the woods.

5

"Come on, *Emily*." I whined without shame.

"Mom's working, she won't hear you," Em said. We had a thing. When she came to my place, she put a layer over her belly tops, talked only about school and pretended she didn't know guys existed. When I went to hers, I called her Emily instead of Em to score extra brownie points with her mom. Her mom named her after Emily Murphy, the first female magistrate in Canada and one of the Famous Five suffragettes who got women qualified as people in the country. She hated that Em shortened it. In addition to using Em's full name, I also talked about feminism when in common rooms and assured Em's mom that I was headed for a STEM career. According to Em's mom, it was important for women to represent in Science, Technology, Engineering, and Mathematics. According to Ma too – she insisted smart women caught better husbands.

"I don't understand, Ya-ya." Em used her nickname for me, which sounded silly but I'd had worse nicknames, so I let it slide.

She led the way to her room wearing a lavender tank top and light blue jean cutoffs – she only kept up the goth-esque shtick at school "Why do *you* want to call *him*?"

I'd been so sick with worry about Michael for the last couple of hours, I'd been drowning in regret over leaving him there. The blood on the woman's head had been dark. Like it had time to dry, but still. What if the murderer came back and found Michael there?

Even when I convinced myself Michael was safe, I couldn't stop thinking about the woman? Who was she? What happened to her? Was she still lying out there alone?

Unable to stand it any longer, I'd asked to go over to Em's house. Since she lived with her physicist single mother (yay, higher education!), she had no brothers (yay, Satanic sex virus free zone!), and my parents would jump at the chance to adopt Em (yay, operation get-each-others'-parents-to-love-us), I had a free pass to go to Em's house whenever, as long as my homework was done.

Em swiped away the white mesh curtain trailing from the canopy covering her bed and plopped down on the pink satin coverlet. "You do know it's supposed to be the other way around, right?"

I didn't know anything about dating rules and I didn't care. I just wanted to know that Michael was okay.

"He can't call me, so I came here to call him," I said. "You're the one who's always telling me he's into me. You sent him to me this morning. And now you won't help me?"

"Oh, I'll help you," Em said. "As soon as you tell me what happened during your walk in the woods."

Em had been the one who'd explained to me that the song "Cake by the Ocean" was about sex on the beach. The way she said 'walk in the woods' with a smirk on her face made me wonder if it was a euphemism for sex against trees.

"Spill it already!" Em bounced up and down on the bed. "And don't leave anything out."

I'd thought about it on my way over here, whether to tell Em about the body. I wanted to. Em was totally loyal to me… unless she had the opportunity to get time with a guy *for me*. If Em had told Michael where I'd be even though she knew how much trouble I'd get in if I got caught, I could just imagine her conversation with the police:

"You're not going to get anything out of me!" Em would yell in my defence. "You think I don't know what'll happen to my best friend if I talk?"

"I'd have to take her downtown." The officer would say.

"Would you really?" Em would ask, clasping her fingers together at the side of her neck. "Because she totally deserves the best. This is everything you need to know…."

Not that the police would say that since Sheriden doesn't really have a downtown. And not that the police had any reason to come for me. I hoped.

"Well?" Em asked.

"We just walked," I said.

"Boring!"

"And talked about stuff."

"What stuff?"

That he wanted to hang out with me. That I couldn't because I'm blah. That he lives on his own like an actual adult because he's the opposite of blah. But I couldn't tell Em that part so I just gave her what she wanted to hear.

"He touched my hair," I said.

"How?"

"He moved a strand off my face, behind my ear."

Em nodded. "A good start. What else?"

"He held my hand." I offered, leaving out the part where it only happened for about three seconds before I freaked.

"Yeah?" Em asked. "That's really romantic."

"Yeah." I nodded, waiting for the part where she got to making the call.

"Is that a blush on your cheeks?"

I didn't think there was, but it couldn't hurt. I turned up the bashful. "I guess, yeah."

"Wow," Em shook her head smiling, "he must give really good hand to have you this wound up."

I was about to nod again. "Ye– Wait. What?"

"Stop shitting me, Ya-ya! There is no way you're dying to talk to him now when you saw him a few hours ago and you'll see him in school tomorrow. Just because he touched your hair and held your hand? I don't think so." Em crossed her arms. "Tell me what really happened. I'm not making the call until you do."

"Fine!" I said, accepting there was no way Em would make the call until she got her romance fix. "We kissed."

"Oh my God! Oh my God! Oh my God!" Em jumped up and down. She didn't actually believe in God, but she liked the phrase plenty when she got excited. "How did it happen?"

She needed a story to go with it too? Okay. "We were racing and I fell."

"Aww, did he come down beside you and kiss you then?"

Beside a dead woman? "No! He, um, waited for me to get up, and then he took my arm and walked me away. Far away from there. And he walked me all the way back to the Centre. Then he kissed me."

"That's a little weird, but okay!" Em's excitement could not be bound. "Wait! Did he kiss you with or without tongue?"

I figured more is better so I went with, "With."

"Right off the bat?"

"Yeah," I said. "It was totally… tongue-y"

"I really thought Michael would be smoother than that." Em's expression looked something between confused and 'I just ate something sour.' She got over it quickly, her eyes getting dreamy again in an instant. "What did it feel like?"

I tried to imagine what Michael's tongue would feel like against mine. "Slimy?"

"Oh, don't worry. It's always a little weird at first. But you get used to it and then it just gets better and better."

"I can't wait." I picked up her cell phone and put it in her hand. "I'm just dying to hear his voice again."

"I really don't think this is a good idea," Em said, but she unlocked her phone and started dialling. "You should wait for him to call you or he'll think you're desperate."

I was desperate.

She put the phone to her ear. "The only reason I'm doing this is because I know he's totally into you too."

I bit my lip as I waited, listening to the phone drone on.

"I got his voicemail," Em said in a rush. "Should I leave a message?"

"Yes. Tell him to call me. I mean you," I said. "Make sure he knows it's urgent."

Em nodded and spoke at the beep. "Hey Michael, it's Em calling with your girl Asiya here."

I rolled my eyes, and waved my hand for her to get to it.

"It would be really cool if you could call us back. Soon. On my phone, of course," Em said. "Oh, and Michael? When I told you where she was, I didn't expect you to go devour her, you oaf! Who slips a girl his tongue on her first kiss, huh?"

"Em!" I swiped at the phone in her hand.

She lurched back on the bed and I leaned over to grab at the phone but she pulled away, gave me a cheeky smile and said, "Lucky for you, she didn't mind."

Unable to reach the phone from where I was, I sat on her. By the time I got it, Em had hung up.

"What did you do!"

"I reminded him he needs to treat you like the precious gift that you are." She cuffed me in the kidneys. "Now get your cement ass off me."

"You weren't supposed to tell anyone!" I took my time moving off of her, and might have dug a knee into her side on my way.

"Anyone else." Em sat up with a hand rubbing her side and a 'duh' look on her face. "Michael already knew. Remember?

He's the one who had his tongue in your face, who you can't wait to see again!"

6

Ma stood at the stove, flipping *porota*, a pan-fried bread that was crispy on the outside and had soft, thin roti layers on the inside. She simultaneously slid the *porota* onto a plate ready with a tomato, onion, and chilli pepper omelette while tossing the next *porota* into the pan and yelling, "Adil, food's ready!"

She must have used the eyes in the back of her head to see me, because she asked, "You want *porota*?" without turning.

It smelled delicious, but I decided to pass on fried food first thing in the morning. "No, thanks. I'm going to have oatmeal."

I'd bugged Em all evening after returning from her house yesterday. Michael hadn't responded. Knowing it was coming, she'd texted me before I could ask this morning.

Em: *Still no word =(*

I went about heating my oatmeal, slicing bananas,

sprinkling brown sugar, and counting down the seconds until I could leave for school. I couldn't wait to see for myself that Michael was alright and someone had come to help that woman. I'd have to make sure Michael was okay from far, far away, of course. After which I'd immediately need to figure out how to hide from him for the rest of the school year.

I put my bowl down on the table next to Adil.

His face scrunched up. "*Apa*, that looks like gruel."

"Don't make fun of my food." I picked out a chunk of brown sugar and lovingly threw it at his face. He tracked and caught it in his mouth like only Adil could, munching the bit of sugar between bites of omelette. "Unlike you, I don't do buffets for breakfast. And lunch. And dinner."

Adil grinned. Until he spotted Abbu shuffle into the kitchen wearing his at-home outfit: a white cotton man-tank, a *lounggi* and slippers.

"Do you have to go get the paper in your *lounggi*?" Adil whined in the direction of the ankle length cloth Abbu had tied at his waist. "All the neighbours will think you're wearing a skirt. Then they'll think I secretly wear skirts at home too."

Abbu raised an eyebrow and laughed. "Then you should be happy."

Adil's brow wrinkled. "That people think I wear skirts?"

"That your father isn't Scottish." Abbu winked at me. "Then the neighbours will think you wear mini-skirts."

Adil groaned and Abbu tapped him on the back of the head with the rolled up paper before dropping it beside him and going over to help Ma at the stove.

"Whoa," Adil said looking down at the front page.

I knew exactly what he was going to say before he said, "There was a murder in Sheriden."

No. Adil, no. I tried to kick him under the table, but of course, his scrawny legs, that were usually sprawled all over the place, were nowhere to be found.

Ma put the wooden spoon she used to flip *porota* down. Abbu turned with her, their full attention on Adil.

I tried to signal with my eyes for Adil to shut up but he didn't see. He was too busy blurting out, "*Apa*, they found a dead body where you work!"

7

Michael, where are you?

I'd started with looking for him from afar. Then I'd stalked him outright, waiting by his locker between classes and asking people he hung out with if they'd seen him. Not only had no one seen him, no one I talked to had heard from him all weekend.

"Wow, Ya-ya, when you finally decide to like a guy, you really go hard at it," Em said. I was momentarily distracted by seeing Em in her big, black, duster again. For a second, I felt like I was at the masjid with women wearing long black abayas.

"He still hasn't called?" I asked, trying not to despair.

Em shook her head, her face losing all trace of joking. "Ya-ya, I know this is your first time but you've got to get it together. Do your thing and he'll be around soon enough."

I wished I could do that, but all I could think about was

Michael as I'd left. He'd been shaking, and scared, and alone thanks to me.

As I navigated through the crowded halls, praying that I would see Michael sitting in his seat in English class, my mind wandered back to breakfast. Which immediately triggered a desire to strangle Adil.

I loved my little brother. I knew he wasn't a dope on purpose. He just didn't get what it was like to have to protect every ounce of freedom he had because as a guy he was afforded way more than I was despite being four years younger.

My fingers curled tight around my books. If I was honest, it wasn't only Adil I was angry at. Thanks to his stupid mouth, I had lied to Ma and Abbu. Repeatedly.

No, I didn't know anything about this.

No, I never go into the woods.

No, I shouldn't quit. The woods are huge, and the body was probably found way on the other side.

All of which made no difference to Ma. She'd already had the phone in her hand, ready to call Nasreen Aunty about me joining her at the masjid soup kitchen.

I'd turned pleading eyes on Abbu and he'd done the best he could. He'd convince Ma to wait through the week and see what details came out before they made a decision. Which made me feel so much worse, because as soon as he was done advocating on my behalf, I'd betrayed him.

"Asiya," Abbu said, his voice soft in the front hallway where I was putting on my shoes. "Talk to me, old friend."

Despite the stress of the morning, Abbu brought out a small smile from me. "Talk to me, old friend," is what Professor

X says to Magneto in the X-men. The two of them basically have the most bromantic frenemyship ever written – hardly mine and Abbu's relationship but Abbu has this running joke that since he was bald and had gifted kids (Afiya and I were in gifted programs and the joke stuck before Adil got to school and they realized he wasn't), Abbu was Professor X from the X-men. I had to strain to imagine myself as a superhero. If anything, I related to Rogue more than anyone else since we both had that no touching boys thing going on.

"I don't know what to say," I said. I was scared that if I said anything, I'd blurt out everything. Which would be horrible because regardless of what he said, Abbu wasn't my friend. He was my parent, the cooler of the two, but still strict by most people's standards.

"Tell me why you are upset," Abbu said.

"I don't want to volunteer in a kitchen." I felt my eyes heat. "I just wanted a chance to learn something outside of books and home and… the masjid."

Abbu gave me a knowing smile. He was a committed member of the community, but wasn't as thrilled with how things were run as Ma was.

"I don't know why Ma has to make every time I go somewhere such a big deal."

"Your Ma has sacrificed her life to stay home and take care of all of you," Abbu said. "And when she goes out, she wears hijab so her experience of how kind people are and how safe it is here will be different than yours."

"I know she sacrificed a lot, and I know it's not easy to be different," I said, trying not to get frustrated. Of all the people who made me feel like I was less than Ma and Afiya for not wearing a hijab, Abbu wasn't one of them. "But I don't want to live the rest of my life like I'm always under the threat of attack."

"I'll do what I can, but I can't promise." He rested a hand on the back of my neck and put his forehead against mine. "I need to know you will be safe."

I nodded.

"Promise me," he said. "Promise me you aren't doing anything that could result in trouble there."

I swallowed. What could I say? I can't? Too late? From now on? There was nothing for me to say but, "I promise."

Abbu kissed a smile against my forehead before letting go. "Salam alaikum Mishty."

Mishty. My *dak nam*. Afiya had been a beautiful baby, so they had nicknamed her Beauty. Following in the same tradition, they had lovingly called me Mutki –which is basically the Bengali equivalent of 'fatty.' The name had fallen away with my baby fat during my mid-teens, but Abbu had always been the exception. He had called me Mishty. His Mishty girl. His sweet girl. His sweet, deceiving daughter.

I shook my head as I approached English class, wishing I could shake off the regret of lying to him. Added to the worry over leaving Michael, and guilt over not doing anything for the woman in the woods, my stomach was churning in a way that didn't bode well for my oatmeal.

I stopped outside class. I couldn't help it. I prayed. *Okay God. I know You can't be thrilled with me right now. And I know You won't want to grant me a favour – not that You're a wish-*

granting genie or anything.

I was always trying to get a better mental picture of God, and now I was hearing Robin Williams sing and seeing the Disney version of the Genie as God. Great.

God, take two please? First, I know You're not Robin Williams and most likely not blue, and I know I haven't been behaving at my best, but I'm asking this not for me but for one of Your creations. Please let Michael be okay?

Okay, never mind. You're too smart to fall for that, and I'm not going to lie to myself. It's for me. Or at least for me too. It would really help me out if you could please resolve this Michael/dead body/parents finding out thing smoothly by just having Michael sitting there safely in English class and the police taking care of the rest of it. Please God, please let everything be okay.

With that prayer that probably had God red (purple?) with anger, I walked into English.

Michael wasn't there.

8

It hit me that Michael was missing and I was the only one who knew. I couldn't wait any longer. He'd been missing for a full day. He might just be skipping – he'd never missed English so far, so that was unlikely – or have the flu. But if I didn't say anything, and something was wrong...

I took a shaky breath as I made my way to my desk. I had to tell someone. After school, I would – who was I kidding? I couldn't explain this to Ma. I wouldn't get five words out before the word "Michael" would instigate an all-out exorcism. I'd have to wait for Abbu. I swallowed. Just a couple extra hours. Abbu would be upset, angry even. But then he'd help me do the right thing.

I'd been so wrapped up in planning my confession, I didn't notice the quiet in the classroom until Mr. Mathis directed us to listen to Principal Wootten. He'd entered the room with a uniformed police officer.

Wootten stepped forward and cleared his throat. "Students, this is Constable Sean Keith. He needs to talk to you about one of our students. This is a very serious matter, so please give him your full attention."

Constable Keith stood as tall as Wootten, but beside Wootten's pumped build, Constable Keith's lanky form and pale skin looked almost malnourished. He had red hair and a freckled face that would have made him look as young as the students in the class if it weren't for the shrewdness in his blue eyes.

"As Principal Wootten said, I'm Constable Keith with the Sheriden Police Department. I'm looking for information on Michael Riley."

I sucked in a breath... at the same moment Constable Keith's gaze flew over the section of the classroom I sat in. His keen eyes caught my surprise and zeroed in on me. My breath caught in my suddenly frozen body. Then, like it never happened, he moved on.

"He seems to be missing as of yesterday evening. I understand he hasn't been in school today. Has anyone here seen or heard from him either today or this weekend?"

This was it. I should tell him now. Before I could say anything, Constable Keith's gaze pinged back to mine. "No one?"

Something about his gaze chilled me. If I told him I'd been with Michael, I would be at his mercy, which he didn't seem to have a shred of.

"I see," Keith said, his eyes assessing.

"Has anyone here been in contact with him outside of school last week?" Keith asked, moving on to pace across the front of the class, his eyes running up and down the rows.

"We played ball together Friday," Bert said.

Constable Keith tilted his head toward the door. "You get out of class free."

Bert stood.

"Anyone else?" Constable Keith asked. He surveyed the class, his roaming eyes flicking to me momentarily before moving on.

I opened my mouth.

"Free trip out of school," Keith said, like he was a game show host making a generous offer.

My mouth snapped shut.

"Grab your books," Constable Keith told Bert. "Might take a while."

My chest thumped. Was he taking Bert to the police station? I could not go to the police station. Ma would cut off volunteering. I wouldn't graduate. And that would only be the beginning.

But Michael was missing. What if Michael was in trouble?

What if he wasn't?

Constable Keith followed Bert to the door.

"Do you think something happened to Michael?" I heard myself ask in a rush.

Six feet of blue uniform stopped mid-step and turned. A laser sharp gaze landed on me.

"What's it to you?" He tilted his head as if to take a closer look. "Are you his girlfriend?"

A few people tittered. They were laughing at how absurd it was that I'd be his, or anyone's girlfriend, but Keith's glare threatened to incinerate them as if they'd affronted him.

"No," I said, feeling my face heat up. I hadn't been anything close to in trouble with an authority other than Ma since the Dunkaroos incident in elementary school. "But he's… you don't have to date someone to want them to be okay."

Keith took his time sauntering over to stand above me. He stood so high above me I had to lean back in my seat and tilt my neck back to see him. "He'll be okay," Keith said, flicking my notebook closed. "If you come tell me what you know."

I could feel myself shrinking under his stare. If I hadn't had so much practice with Ma, I would have broken on the spot. Still, the pressure was enough that I couldn't focus. Something about what Keith said was hitting me wrong and I couldn't figure out what.

"You sure there's nothing you want to tell me?" he asked, his face telling me he already knew the answer.

The way he was talking to me, it wasn't like he was concerned. More like he was angry. Or maybe I was just making excuses not to do the right thing. I was making this worse for myself. I should just tell him.

"Constable Keith, I can assure you Asiya is one of our most responsible students." Principal Wootten shuffled toward us. "Smart girl, studies hard, but not all that social. I know for a fact she's not Michael's girlfriend and hasn't seen him outside of school."

Constable Keith raised an eyebrow at that. "How so?" he asked, still watching me.

"I know her mother from many, many, many visits to the school." Wootten let out a nervous chuckle. "Ballsy lady. I can personally vouch that Asiya's not allowed to have boyfriends or go out with boys and is very diligently supervised on that."

The class laughed out loud despite Keith's glare. I was ready to start banging my flustered face against my desk, but apparently total humiliation wasn't enough for Constable Keith.

"That true?" he asked.

I couldn't believe he was asking me to answer that in front of the entire class but he crossed his arms over his chest, making it clear he wasn't moving until I did. It wasn't like everyone didn't already kind of know it. It was just so much worse to admit it out loud. I nodded my eyes straight ahead, my lips tight.

Keith's hard stare scorched me, but at this point, I didn't care. Five, ten, fifteen seconds passed and just when I thought I'd break down and blurt it all out right there, I heard Constable Keith turn and walk away. But not before he said just for my ears, "I don't tolerate troublemaking brats."

He ushered Bert out the door. Wootten threw me a smile and a big thumbs up before following them out.

The class erupted in noise the moment they left. Mr. Mathis half-heartedly tried to corral the class back into paying attention.

I stared down at my closed book. Not only had Constable Keith embarrassed me in front of everyone, he'd ignored my question. But I could read between the lines:

First, Michael *was* missing.

Second, Constable Keith was the aggressive, trigger-happy kind of cop determined to get his guy.

And between the two: Keith seemed to think *Michael* might be his guy. As in the guy who killed that woman.

9

My feet dragged on the walk home. I'd been running through possible scenarios out of this mess since English class. My first instinct was to stick to the plan before Keith stomped onto the scene: talk to Abbu and then tell the police that I'd been there, Michael had been with me, and he'd been as surprised as I was by the woman's body. My confession would clear him.

Except, then I remembered Michael must have covered for me when he called them – there was no way Constable Cranky would have let me off if he knew I'd been there. So then did it make it worse for Michael if I went and revealed he'd lied to them? And the thing that I couldn't even begin to figure out: what had made Michael take off?

This was too much. There were too many variables and I couldn't play them all out, so I went with what I knew: Michael didn't kill anybody. He had to have called the police for them to connect him to the murder. I had to believe that because otherwise that poor woman's body was still lying there alone, without anyone to lay her to rest, or seek justice for her. And he had to have covered for me as I was presently free instead of holed up in an interrogation room with Constable Keith – I shuddered at the thought. And finally, if I broke Michael's cover for me now, the police would know he had lied about something and could assume he had lied about other things, which would not be good.

I turned onto my street with a deepening thud hitting in my hollow chest. Michael had lied to protect me. Now he was in trouble and I didn't know how to help him other than to say nothing.

The police.

My stride stuttered. My toe stubbed on the sidewalk as my brain channelled all resources to focus in on the Chevy Impala parked at our curb. That particular Impala belonged to our neighbour, Jamie. Technically it belonged to the City of Sheriden, but Jamie drove it when she was working as a detective at the Sheriden Police Department.

My brain farted. At once all these possibilities – none of them ending well – entered my head, annihilating any chance of coherent thought. In order to function, I focused on one: Jamie was one of the good ones.

I was too young to remember, but in the years after 9/11, Muslims were interrogated like they had warts and extra big broom closets during the witch hunt for terrorists. Abbu had been among the many put "on trial." The RCMP had taken him to the Sheriden police station to "question" him. Abbu said it was more like an interrogation that assumed he was guilty, went for hours and didn't seem like it would ever end. But it did end. Because when Jamie heard, she'd gone out of her way to vouch for Abbu. She'd lived down the street from us forever, respected the way Ma and Abbu raised their family, and thought more parents should be like them. She'd told the Mounties as much.

I should have thought to go to her in the first place, but now she was here with Ma. I put my hand on the door knob and paused. I was not ready for this. But since I had nowhere to run, I–

The door yanked open, dragging me in. Ma's scowl greeted me. "What did you do?" she hissed in a whisper low enough not to carry, but harsh enough to kickstart the fear of God in me.

"I don't know," I said, not because I hadn't done anything but because I didn't know where to start.

"Then why are the police here for you?" Ma tilted her head toward the family room and didn't wait for me to answer. "Do not talk, do not argue, do not do anything." She pinned me with her bulgy-eyed 'don't test me' look.

As much as I wanted to obey Ma in this instance, I didn't think I could get away with complete silence with Jamie. On the other hand, Ma seemed to be in a particularly undemocratic mood. No matter how things went with Jamie, I was going to be at Ma's mercy afterward. I kept my mouth shut and followed her into the family room.

"Asiya." Jamie's voice was friendly but her hazel-green eyes lacked her usual neighbourly warmth. The message was clear: this was business. "How are you doing?"

The sight of Jamie in her boxy jacket, just-long-enough-to-tie-back blonde hair, and general police-ish manner eased the stranglehold on my veins. Ma wouldn't go ballistic on me in front of her. Or at least I hoped. Despite Jamie's presence, I said a quick prayer, asking God for help to get through this. In that moment, I needed reassurance that someone had more power than Ma.

"Umm, I'm okay," I said, noticing the furniture was covered. Ma kept her couches pristine by covering them with old sheets. She had us scrambling around the house to strip them off and chuck them into a closet just before we had guests. Jamie had showed up unexpected.

"I don't want you to be scared." Jamie gave me an encouraging look. "You're not in trouble."

I didn't say anything. I was already in trouble with Ma, and I was pretty sure that could change quick with Jamie.

"I'm sure you heard Michael Riley is missing?" Jamie watched me carefully. "He's a student at your school."

"My daughter does not talk to boys," Ma said at the same time that I said, "What happened to Michael?"

Ma glared at me and I regretted doubting her wisdom about staying quiet.

Jamie caught the glare. "Khushie," she missed the 'h' and pronounced my mom's name *Koo-she*, "I know this is nerve-wracking, having the police stop by your place, but I also know you've done a great job raising your kids. Asiya is not in trouble. I just want to ask her some questions."

Ma nodded, ceding to Jamie's flattery.

Jamie turned sincere eyes on me. "We hope nothing happened to him. And we certainly don't want anything bad to happen to him either. I'm guessing you know him?"

"I go to school with him." I glanced at Ma. "We have English class together."

Just as I was recalling the disaster that was English class today, I heard the toilet flush in the hallway bathroom, the water run and the door open.

The next thing I knew, Constable Keith was towering over me, glaring down at me in my own house.

10

We're going to catch him sooner or later," the quite likely constipated Constable said. Seriously how long had he been in the washroom? "You might as well stop covering for your boyfriend."

"Asiya!?!" Ma's panicked voice shrilled at the same time I yelled, "He's not my boyfriend!"

I faced Ma and repeated. "I do not have a boyfriend."

"Keith." Jamie's voice was very different than the one she used with Ma or me. It was a harsh, sharp reprimand followed with a tilt of her head commanding him to sit. Despite my turmoil, I couldn't help feeling a little smug at watching him obey. Except as he stiffly lowered himself to the couch he was watching me. The way his eyes narrowed said he could tell what I was thinking. And that he would get retribution for it.

I focused on Jamie, where it was safer. "What does he

mean, by 'catch Michael'?"

"Keith is getting ahead of himself," Jamie said tightly. "We're hoping this is all just a misunderstanding." Keith snorted and Jamie's lips tightened, but continued. "We need help to clear up what happened to him. Would you know anything about that?"

At that moment, Adil scuttered in the front door, dumped his backpack on the floor, dropped his jacket on top, kicked off his shoes, one of them pattering halfway down the entryway toward us. Right then, I'd never loved my spoiled, sloppy, video game-addicted baby brother more. He yelled a general, "Salam alaikum!" and made it halfway to the basement door before he realized something was off and peeked into the family room. His eyes widened at Ma's angry expression, and me sitting with Jamie and a uniformed cop.

"What's going on?" Adil stepped into the room. "Are they trying to arrest Apa?"

"Adil," Ma said in that way that only required her to say our names in order to convey whatever command she was dictating at the moment and whatever future threat was implied if we didn't follow through.

Adil knew it well. He held up his palms. "Okay, fine. I'm gone."

We watched him skip down the basement stairs. A few seconds later the sound of electric guitars, bullets shooting and Adil yelling, "Oh yeah? You wanna try me? I will slice you like salami!" wafted up the stairs.

I jumped up and shut the basement door, grateful for the excuse to get away from the suffocating air in the family room, even for a couple seconds. I held onto the knob a few extra moments before forcing myself back in front of the firing squad.

In the time it took me to get back, Ma had decided to switch sides. "Asiya is a good girl," she said, directing her stony ire toward Jamie as well, but mostly Keith for putting my name and the word 'boyfriend' in a sentence together. "She does not mix with boys." Ma insisted. "She knows nothing of this Michael."

Ma said Michael's name with the kind of disdain that a woman who demanded perfect obedience from her kids had for other people's kids who dared have problems. I didn't know whether to be grateful for Ma's defence of me, or cringe at her smugness.

"No one doubts that Asiya is a good kid," Jamie said, a little shortly.

"Are you kidding me?" Keith asked in a crabby voice that indicated despite his trip to the bathroom, he still had something up his butt. I pushed away the nudge of guilt insisting that something was the knowledge that I was lying. He was halfway up from the couch, directing an incredulous hand in my vicinity. "You can't be in that much denial about your kid."

Ma didn't like his tone any more than I did. She was up to her full 5'2" in a heartbeat. "If my daughter saw that boy she would lower her gaze!"

Between Keith's certainty I was a criminal groupie, Ma's conviction I had one up on virginal saints, and my need to cover for Michael, I felt trapped to do or say anything.

"Lady, you're crazy if you believe that." Keith stood at his full six plus feet. He stepped toward Ma. "Now let's cut the perfect little girl bullshit, because we have—"

"Get away from her." I was between Keith and Ma before I knew it. "Or so help me God."

"Keith." Jamie's insistent voice felt like it came from far away.

Keith ignored her warning and took another step, right into what should have been my personal space.

I vaguely noticed Ma tugging at my shoulder, urging me away but I focused on the Goliath before me.

"What are you going to do?" Keith smirked. "Lower your gaze?"

My face was red. I was shaking. My neck strained from staring up at him from this close range. I had no idea what I'd do if Keith didn't back down, but I couldn't let him talk to Ma like that. It was one thing to tower over me with that incinerating glare, but Ma was... domestic. All she wanted was to build her safe perfect world at home. Keith thought he could come into our house and ruin that for her?

I pulled my phone from my pocket. "How about I add a few hundred gazes instead? Or do you think thousands of people would be interested in seeing a cop bully women a foot shorter than him once I post this online? What do you think?"

Keith's eyes raged. His nostril's flared. His mouth opened and even before sound came out I knew I was going to get skewered. "I am going to—"

"That's enough." Jamie's sharp voice cut over Keith's and through my red haze. "Keith. Unless you want me to recommend putting you back on patrol, you're going to go back to the car immediately."

Keith glared at Jamie. "You're going to let them–"

"I'm not going to do anything but have a bit of tact." Jamie scowled back, looking impressively ferocious. "Now what's it going to be?"

Keith's raging eyes moved from me to Jamie and for a second I thought he'd pick tearing me apart over his fledgling career. Then he shook his head, mumbled something about criminals in the making under his breath, and he took off.

I wilted at the sight of his retreating back and the sound of him leaving the house. My relief only lasted a moment.

"Khushie, if you don't want to accompany me to the police station to question Asiya there, you're going to let her walk me to the door."

Ma's eyes widened. There was no way people she knew wouldn't hear about a visit to the police station in a city as small as Sheriden. I could see her cherished reputation war with parental duty for an instant before duty won. Her mouth opened.

I lay a hand on her arm. "Ma, it's okay. I'll be fine." Before she could register an objection, I hurried with Jamie to the front door.

"I'll make this quick," Jamie said in a hushed voice. "You're friends with Michael."

I nodded.

She sought something in my face as she said. "Maybe you're more."

I felt my eyes widen involuntarily. How was it possible she

knew? I didn't even know.

"That's what you're hiding." Jamie nodded like she'd known all along. "I'm sorry about all this. I'll make sure Keith doesn't bother you anymore."

"Jamie?" She turned, one hand on the door. "Why does Keith think Michael is a criminal?"

Jamie's surveyed me so long I was sure she was about to remind me I was a kid, she was the police, and I needed to butt out. But then her eyes softened and for just a moment she looked almost maternal.

"You're sweet to worry about your friend." Jamie looked back to where Ma was no doubt listening. When she turned back to me, her professional face had returned. "But you're better off not getting involved."

It was a little late for that.

"Keith seems to think Michael is guilty of something… and I know there was a murder recently," I said. "He can't think Michael had anything to do with that."

Jamie didn't respond.

"Does he?"

Jamie's lips pursed ever so slightly as she contemplated me. "Asiya, I'm going to tell you something – something for your ears only – so you understand how serious it is that you stay away from the situation."

I appreciated Jamie trying to prep me, but I already knew that Michael had found the body and didn't have an alibi. This would be the perfect time to tell someone he did. That he had nothing to do with killing that woman and I knew, because I was with him.

"Michael was seen entering the deceased's apartment."

"What?" I gasped. I felt my head shaking in denial. Why would he… "There's no way."

"A neighbour saw him and called it in."

"Maybe it was someone else," I said.

"It was him. The neighbour identified him by name," Jamie said. "He'd been there before."

"No." There was no way what I was hearing could be true. But even as I thought it, I remembered Michael's shock at seeing the woman. *He'd known her.*

"Yes, Asiya," Jamie said kindly but firmly. "When the officer tried to apprehend him, Michael ran. I know you were raised to be helpful and I appreciate that you befriended someone with a different upbringing than you, but getting involved with Michael would be misguided."

What did that mean? Did Michael's foster care records show a history of causing trouble? He'd told me as much himself. But how was I supposed to know that included breaking into dead people's apartments? I mean, why would he… I held in a cackle of anxious laughter. Stupid me, I'd thought he'd been sweet offering to cover for me. But really he'd been in a rush to get rid of me so he could get on with robbing a dead woman.

"If you know what's good for you," Jamie's eyes flicked back to the family room, "you'll stay away from him."

That would not be a problem. It didn't matter if he was guilty of murder, robbery or just making me feel like stupid scum on the bottom of his shoe. From here on out, I was done with Michael.

11

Just because two things collide, doesn't mean there'll be a change. They could collide with the right amount of energy, and there could still be no change. Only when they collide with sufficient energy and the right orientation do bonds break, and possible reactions occur.

I heaved a sigh and dropped my pencil like it was what had me feeling so heavy. My Chemistry homework wasn't the culprit either. So far collision theory was pretty clear and notetaking was going fine. I just couldn't sit any longer. Four days had gone by since Keith's threat, and Jamie's extraction of a promise that I'd call her if I heard from Michael, and I was still humming.

I was so desperate for something more physically demanding than homework, I went down to see if Ma needed help making dinner. Or maybe I was just grateful Ma hadn't held the police visit against me.

I had Keith's macho dramatics to thank for that. He'd painted Michael as a hardcore criminal and as much as Ma worried I was going astray with my every next breath, even she didn't believe I was secretly involved with a murderer. She'd been only too happy to hate on Keith and even remarked that he had Satan in his eyes. Mostly I tried to gently discourage Ma's generalizations of people, but this time I totally and vocally agreed.

In the kitchen, Ma was sitting at the table cutting green beans. Her best friend Nasreen Aunty was sorting through a bowl of lentils. Both women had steaming cups of tea beside them as they chatted. Nasreen Aunty came over multiple times a week for discussions on the on-goings of people in the Bengali and/or masjid community. It sounded a lot like gossip to me, but they considered it important community work. I could vaguely hear fragments of Nasreen Aunty's son Tariq smack talking and blowing things up with Adil downstairs.

"Salam alaikum, Aunty," I said, as was expected of me to greet my elder.

"Wa alaikum salam, Asiya," Nasreen Aunty said. "How is school?"

"Good," I said, even though that was a pretty far stretch from reality. But it wasn't like I was going to tell her that each day was a nerve-wracking wait to see whether Michael would show up or not. And that it was awkward hearing people who were supposed to be Michael's friends speculate about his involvement in the murder.

I washed my hands, grabbed the peeler and picked up one

of the potatoes Ma had out. Within moments Nasreen Aunty did what Nasreen Aunty does.

"Oh, Asiya. You peel with such a heavy hand." She sipped her tea and nodded to the white flesh lining the scraps in front of me.

I continued peeling, determined to tune her out, except that she said, "Do not worry. I'll teach you to peel without wasting so much potato when you come to the masjid kitchen."

My eyes, wide with surprise and a plea for mercy, swung to Ma. I'd thought we'd been good. I'd made sure to be especially good, helping her with dinner and housework around doing my homework all week.

Ma shrugged a shoulder, as if to ask how I'd expected any different. She nodded toward the paper I hadn't noticed sitting to one side of the table. "That social worker. She was found dead near to your volunteer place. You cannot go back there."

The potato and peeler dropped from my hands. I grabbed the paper and scanned the article. Her name was Sue Murray. The woman I'd thought was a log. I'm sorry Sue. The woman I'd tripped over was now a person… a social worker with Sheriden Child Services. An alarm, loud and pervasive, went off in my head. The woman whose body Michael and I had found, whose apartment Michael had broken into and been to before, worked in child services? The woman who was dead, just weeks after Michael came to town looking for his parents? I needed to think this through, but not while I could feel Ma and Nasreen Aunty watching me.

"I need to run." I implored Ma. "Around the neighbourhood, please?"

Ma hesitated. "You should not go alone." Her gaze fell to the paper in front of me. "There is a murderer in our city."

"Hai, hai, what has Sheriden come to?" Nasreen Aunty tutted three times quickly. "It is just as bad now as it was when Mercer was here."

That had me carefully refraining from rolling my eyes. Mercer was a mobster/fraudster/murderer who also dabbled in white collar crime. For some reason, instead of picking a big city, he decided to make this little suburb of a suburb home. Rumour had it he had ruled the city, its streets, and its officials. But he'd been dead since before I was born and this one murder did not mean organized crime was back in the city. "Ma, it's day time. There are kids" riding tricycles "outside still."

Ma's face showed she obviously leaned toward Nasreen Aunty's crime and chaos interpretation of things.

"Please, Ma." I pressed a palm to my stomach. "If I don't exercise, I'm going to gain weight."

"This much is true," Nasreen Aunty said, glancing over my thighs, "Afiya and my Rina were never this healthy." Of course, by 'healthy' (pronounced hell-thee), Nasreen Aunty meant fat. It was Bengali code, the kind that wasn't a secret because you said it to people's faces. Like the way people said "bless your heart" but everyone including the person they said it to knew it really meant "shrivel up and die," or something like that.

I patiently reminded myself that the circumference of my thighs had as much to do with muscle as it did fat. And that Nasreen Aunty's life was the stuff of my personal nightmares, so I should feel sorry for her. I focused on silently pleading with Ma since too much verbal imploring could be construed as backtalk.

She sighed. "Atcha, go. But take Adil and Tariq with you."

"Ma, no!" Adil and Tariq were hardcore gamers who thought butt-on-the-couch marathons to defeat fantasy enemies were the height of determination. The sound of explosions and a gaggle of laughter burst from downstairs. "They're playing their game and anyway, they slow me down."

"You are a girl," Nasreen Aunty said. "You have no need to run faster than the boys."

That made no sense so once again I didn't bother responding. Unfortunately, Ma seemed to agree with that nonsense because she went to the basement door and yelled for Adil and Tariq to come up.

They trampled up the stairs like a stampede of geriatric elephants.

I got a "Hey Apa," from Adil and "Hey," from Tariq.

"Your Apa wants to go to run," Ma said. "Go with her."

"But we were just about to rip out Herobrine's heart!" Adil whined.

Ma dismissed that with a wave of her hand. "Later. Go run now."

***

I usually felt bad when Adil – and sometimes, by extension Tariq – got dragged into doing things with me, but today I was too desperate to get out to care. I turned to look over my shoulder at them, now trailing a full block behind me. We hadn't finished warming up and they were already winded.

I pulled up to the park at the corner of the next street and jogged in place as I waited for them. Tariq bent and grabbed his legs as soon as he reached me. A little later, Adil announced he'd made it as well by swinging his arms around my neck and hanging off of me. "Apa, I'm dying. And not survival mode death where you keep coming back. Hardcore mode death where not only the hero dies, but the whole world ends after him."

"You'll be okay." I grunted as I drag-walked my brother over to a bench and dropped him. "How about you guys stay here while I finish my run? I'll come back and get you when I'm done."

"Deal." Adil sprawled out on the bench, his head hanging back. Tariq looked like he wanted to say something, but I didn't bother waiting to hear it. I'd already had enough from his mother. I took off with a "See-ya," knowing that once I was gone they wouldn't dare tell. They'd be in as much trouble as I would for us separating. It was a curious thing about Bengali mothers. It was like as soon as they started disciplining they couldn't stop until all the kids in the general vicinity had the fear of God (or at least the women doing the disciplining) back in them.

I inhaled steady breaths as I ran, relaxing into my stride and feeling the sense of relief I'd been looking for since Keith and Jamie left our house. It wasn't even the police visit – although I thoroughly hoped never to have that experience again – that still bothered me. It was what Abbu said to me after Ma had gone off to fold laundry that night.

"Adil told me you defended your Ma very courageously."

I hadn't realized Adil had seen, but I wished he hadn't.

Then Abbu wouldn't be thanking me for doing a tiny bit to fix something that was totally my fault. I'd insisted it was nothing, but I couldn't deter Abbu's praise. Finally, he'd kissed my forehead with a last, "I'm proud of you," before leaving me to wallow in guilt for lying to him over something as stupid as a guy. One who'd lied to me.

Michael had known Sue. He'd wanted to get rid of me after we'd found her. It hadn't escaped me that Jamie had said he'd entered, not broken and entered. He had to have taken Sue's key off her dead body.

As gross as it was, I wanted to believe Michael had robbed a dead woman, because I couldn't stand the alternative, that Michael had... my body tightened messing up my gait. I forced myself to breathe. To remember that I didn't owe Michael anything. Other than a few friendly conversations, eyes that drew me in and fingers that made my skin tingle, I didn't really know him. And I did know that he'd lied to me about a lot.

The niggling feeling from the kitchen came back, this time coming to a full-fledged idea: what if Michael has been pursuing finding his parents through Sue and she'd refused?

Michael not only lied to me, he knew Sue, and he had a reason to kill her. A car stopped at the entrance to the plaza in front of me, waiting for the road to clear so it could turn. I jogged on the spot as I waited for it to clear the sidewalk but my arms and legs moved lethargically as my mind finally processed what I hadn't let it all week: Michael really might have murdered Sue.

And I –I had told my parents and the police I hadn't seen him. Or her.

The woman. The dead body. The log I had tripped over. She'd been a person. Her name was Sue, and I might have helped Michael get away with killing her.

I couldn't breathe. My vision refocused to see the car had cleared and the road was empty. I staggered forward, unable to do more than focus on putting one foot slowly in front of the other.

I heard another jogger behind me and moved aside to let the person pass. Footsteps thudded closer. And then someone was grabbing my arm.

I screamed. A hand clamped my mouth. An arm circled my waist, cinching me against a body much stronger than mine. No matter how much I struggled, I couldn't stop from being dragged behind the plaza.

12

I yelled under the hand on my mouth. My eyes searched for someone, anyone to help me. I saw no one but a feral cat scampering along the high wood fence that separated the plaza from the residences behind it.

I pushed and elbowed and kicked. And then my feet lifted off the floor and didn't come back down until we were completely hidden behind a dumpster. He was talking to me. Saying something urgently, but I couldn't hear beyond my heart thudding in my chest, my throat, my ears. I panted and struggled, fighting the arms and especially the thoughts; the ones that said I was a girl, I couldn't be strong enough. I couldn't get away.

"Asiya! Asiya, stop, please! It's me, Asiya. It's me."

Michael? I froze. The moment I stopped fighting, the arms were gone. I scrambled back, pressed up against the fence, my fingers gripping the wood behind me.

"Michael." He looked scruffy. His face haggard. He lifted a hand.

I scrambled to the side, away from the dumpster and away from him, my eyes gauging the distance between us. My body tensed, ready to run if he came any closer.

"Are you," Michael stared at me, bewilderment in his eyes, "scared of me?"

I gulped in air, hoping it would help calm my heartbeat and help me think. Whatever he dragged me back here for, it probably wasn't a good idea to aggravate him.

I shook my head but Michael saw through it.

"What did they tell you about me?"

"Who?" I tried.

"The police." Michael sneered. "They must have said something because the last time I saw you we'd been getting along pretty damn well."

"Yeah, well you did just grab me and drag me into a back alley." I crossed my arms in front of me. I didn't know if I did it to put on a front of toughness for Michael or if I was trying to comfort myself. "And actually, the last time I saw you, you lied to me about not knowing the dead woman we'd stumbled on."

I tripped on the word 'stumbled,' making it obvious I wasn't sure finding her was actually accidental.

"Asiya, no matter what they said, you have to believe me. I didn't kill Sue." Michael said Sue's name in such a familiar way. His eyes softened. "And I'm sorry I scared you. I just wanted to talk to you, but you screamed and I panicked."

"You didn't call the police like you said you would." I

accused. "You stole her key and went to her apartment to rob her instead."

"That's what you think?" Michael hummed with agitated energy and visibly worked to calm himself. "I told you I came to Sheriden to find my birth parents. Sue was the worker who placed me when I was a baby and I'd been trying to get her to help me for weeks. I could tell she wanted to, that she was close to giving in, but then we found her. I was just as surprised as you were."

Michael's lips tightened and he took a slow breath through his nose, "She was a good person and it killed me to go through her pockets for her keys, but I had to search her apartment. She was the last lead – the only link – I had to my parents."

"If you weren't there to take anything, why did you run?" I asked. "Now the police think you had something to do with her murder."

"They wouldn't have believed me anyway." Michael raised an arm to the back of his neck. "I… When I told you I got into trouble back in Toronto." Michael took a deep breath. "It was with the police."

Of course. Now that I was alone in a back alley with him, he wanted to tell me about his criminal past.

"What kind of trouble are we talking about?" I asked, praying for my sake it wasn't a previous murder charge.

Michael's gaze dropped to the ground before coming back to me, pleading. "Robbery."

Before I knew it, I'd backed up, putting more space between Michael and me.

"It's not like that! I broke into my social worker's car."

"And that's supposed to be okay?" I asked.

"She had my file," Michael said, his face losing all trace of regret. "It's how I found Sue."

He'd already been convicted of robbery. No wonder Keith thought Michael was there to rob Sue. And if they thought he could rob her, they'd think he… he was making this worse for himself. "You have to turn yourself in."

"No way." Michael's face hardened. "Police hate me. They'll look for a way to pin her death on me."

"My neighbour, Jamie, she's a detective, but she's not like the rest of them," I said, thinking of Keith. "She'll listen."

"I said, no." The steel that backed Michael's words didn't leave any room for discussion.

"If they catch you, you'll be in so much more trouble."

"I don't care," Michael said so adamantly I couldn't help but believe him. His determination tugged at me. What was it like to be so desperate to find your family that you'd be willing to approach a dead body and get arrested, just for the possibility of getting a single clue closer to them?

"I need to get into Sue's apartment before they pack it away," Michael said. "Do you understand, Asiya? This is my last chance to find out who my parents are."

Since pulling me into the alley, Michael had let me put more and more space between us. Now, for the first time since letting me go, he stepped in closer. "Asiya. I need you to help me."

"What?" I sputtered. "No. I can't get involved."

"Because you don't believe me."

"I don't know what to believe," I said. "It would have been

easier to believe you if you'd told me you knew Sue. Or that you had a criminal record. Or if you hadn't sent me running while you lifted keys from a dead woman's pockets."

"I wanted to." Michael ran a hand through his hair and clenched at it. "I wanted to tell you all of it, even before we found Sue. I wanted to tell you everything about me. I wanted to ask you to help me search for them."

"Now I know you're making stuff up," I said, starting to get angry. He was using how I felt about him to manipulate me. "You're wrong. I can't help you with this."

"And you're lying to yourself," Michael said. "You act like you're totally incapable, but did you ever stop to think, why not you? You're smart. I mean, you figured out I was after the key on your own, didn't you?"

"I didn't put together that you wanted it to look for things about your parents."

Michael scuffed at something on the ground. "That's because you stopped trusting me."

I blinked. "You say that like I knew you well to begin with! We've had exactly one conversation without Em–"

Michael looked up then, his eyes full with emotion. "Not because I didn't want to."

I took a deep breath and tried again. "Just because you decided you wanted to hang out with me one day–"

"That wasn't the first day I looked for you." Michael's eyebrows raised to mirror mine. "Ask Em if you don't believe me." His eyes fell away. "At the risk of sounding like a stalker, that was the third week I'd gone walking the trails hoping to run into you."

The volume on my heartbeat suddenly turned way up and it had nothing to do with fear. The combination of sweetness and insecurity coming off Michael was twisting my fickle heart. How could I go from thinking he could be a killer a few minutes ago to feeling warm and glowy at his words? For just a piece of a moment, the idea popped into my head: Satan. It had to be. Why else would I, a reasonably rational human being, want to risk everything to help Michael right now?

"Michael, even if I wanted to…"

He took my hand and placed a key in it. Sue's key.

I shook my head, trying to give it back. "I don't want this."

His fingers folded mine, closing them around his last bit of hope. He held my fist in the warmth of his hands. "I know. And I'm sorry to ask you this but the police are looking for me. They'll spot me if I even go near there and I'll lose any chance of finding out who I am."

"Michael…" He was crazy for thinking I could accomplish what he couldn't. My heart bled for him. I wanted him to find his parents, to get whatever he needed to be happy, but I couldn't do this.

"I have no one else to ask," Michael said. "Help me. Asiya. Please. I can see that you want to."

I did. And he could. I just hoped he didn't use that to make me do the wrong thing.

13

"Allah has made man the *khalifah* on earth. The role of the *khalifah* is to apply the orders of Allah, the Most High, in our earthly realm." Imam Alwanee's voice boomed through the speaker system over the masjid.

Like every other Saturday, families filled the carpeted rows. The men sat in the front, the women occupied the back behind a waist high divider, and the really young kids ran blissfully free in the no man (or woman)'s land in between.

"Alweenie probably thinks the verse about *khalifah* was written just for him." Firdous scowled. She had lived in Saudi Arabia most of her life and had been ecstatic when her family moved to a country free of the *Mutaween*, the Saudi modesty police. Since Imam Alwanee and some of the other "brothers" at the *masjid* had ratted Firdous out to her parents for wearing short skirts and hanging out with boys at university, Firdous,

Leyan and I had started calling them the Mutaweenies. Their leader, Imam Alwanee, became Imam Alweenie. And they had continued to suck so the names stuck.

Usually, the three of us suffered Alweenie wisdom together, but I was so occupied with what to do about Michael, I barely participated.

"Tell us what's wrong." Leyan had mastered whispering with barely any movement of her lips. We had to be careful of Nasreen Aunty, who was the self-appointed Mutaweenie of the women's side. Leyan nudged me. "It's like you're concentrating on what Alweenie's saying."

I always listened to what he said with one ear in case Ma brought up something he talked about. I assured Leyan I was just tired. Exhausted really, from trying to figure out what to do. I mean there wasn't anything to do, I just could not enter Sue's apartment for Michael. No matter what it meant to him. My mind got that, but something else in me, something much stupider kept holding out on the idea that I not only would, but should. I noticed that same stupid voice was silent when I considered whether I could actually get away with it.

After an eternity of mental gymnastics as Alweenie droned on, he wrapped up his lecture and someone stood to make the call to prayer. We lined up side by side to pray together as Alweenie led, reciting out loud. I didn't know if it was a coincidence or something more, but one of the chapters he chose was a small one I knew from the end of the Quran called Small Favours. I translated in my head as he crooned in Arabic.

Have you seen the one who denies the moral way of life?
The one who pushes aside the orphan and doesn't

encourage feeding the poor. So a warning to those who pray – the ones who are careless in their devotions – who do good only to be seen, and who refuse to share even the smallest of favours.

The congregation prostrated. This position was supposed to be when God was closest to us, when we supplicated humbly with our foreheads on the ground. I decided this was as good a time as any to ask for clarification.

So God, I could really use some help. You see, I'm not too great with this signs business. Like I've got this itchy, irritating feeling in my chest, but I'm not sure if You're telling me something or it's my dinner coming back up because my stomach is currently higher than my head. Ma's fish curry pushing its way past my stomach sphincter and back up my esophagus would do that too, You know? So could You please, please help me out by making it really, really clear what the right thing to do is in this case?

I came out of prostration, completed the rest of the prayer and made it all the way home looking for God Signs, but seeing none. It was hours later and that feeling in my chest hadn't dulled at all. I didn't know if it was bad indigestion, God giving me a sign, or Satan after me because of alone time in the alley with Michael, but at this point it didn't matter because I'd made my decision.

It wasn't a small favour, but it was for someone who was completely alone in the world. I wasn't going to be the kind of person who wouldn't help.

14

My parents had this weird relationship where they considered Abbu the leader of the family, but Ma the leader of the household. Usually that meant Ma was in charge everything to do with everything other than making money. Abbu didn't seem to mind. Except on the extremely rare occasion when Abbu stepped in and overruled Ma. She allowed it, but she really did mind. Like now, when Abbu had just pissed her off royally by overruling her no-volunteering-other-than-with-Nasreen-Aunty-at-the-*masjid* decree.

"I'm sorry Ma's angry at you because of me," I said, as Abbu drove us to the Conservation Centre.

"What did you think of Imam Alwanee's lecture yesterday?" Abbu asked.

"It was okay?" I asked, unsure what the abrupt change of topic was about.

"Imam Alwanee talked about *khalifah* like it was men who are specifically given the right to rule over everyone else but *khalifah* doesn't have to mean "man." And it doesn't have to be about policing people. It can be about responsibility to do what's best on earth. This can include people, animals, and the planet."

I nodded, understanding what Abbu was getting at.

"Your Ma tends to take literal interpretations like Imam Alwanee."

I always watched Abbu closely to see if he'd slip and say Imam Alwanee's name with a slightest bit of disgust, but he was good. He never gave an inch. Still, I was pretty sure if he ever heard us call the Imam 'Alweenie,' he wouldn't be able to stop himself from laughing. Unfortunately, he'd probably also tell Ma, so I'd never tried.

Abbu pulled up in front of the Conservation Centre. "Your work here is just as much worshipping Allah as working at the masjid. That is the only reason I am allowing you to continue here. And because I know you will stay in the Centre and be safe."

I swallowed, "Sue, the woman who was murdered? She was a social worker who worked with kids. I read that she became a social worker because she was tired of seeing Aboriginal children taken from their families. She seemed like a really good person."

"May Allah reward her for every kindness she gave with kindness in the hereafter."

"You…" I blinked. "Do you believe Allah will reward her with heaven? Even though she's not Muslim?"

"I think that Allah knows better than us the good in people's hearts," Abbu said.

I took off my belt and squeezed him tight. "Thanks, Abbu." Mostly I was thanking him for standing up for me with Ma, but also for making what I was about to do easier. I exited the car and waved, nervously watching him drive off. I needed him gone before I was spotted by someone in the Centre. I'd already emailed Nate that I wasn't coming.

My fingers dug into my pocket and gripped Sue's key. I made a mental note that I owed the planet a good deed, but it would have to be another day because today I had a specific person in mind to help.

After waiting a sufficient amount of time for Abbu to clear the road back, I took off toward Sue's. Google Maps had put her place a half hour walk from the Centre. I had plenty of time to get there, search her apartment and get back before Abbu came to pick me up. I decided to run it anyway. The quicker I got there, the less chance I'd turn around and chicken out.

Sue lived in a short, stout building. It didn't look like the fancy kind that had security – *Thank you God!* – but had a neighbourly feel with flower pots lining people's balconies. I hadn't thought about how I'd get into the building, but I lucked out, arriving just in time to catch the door as a young mother struggled with getting her stroller through. I smiled, holding the door open for her and followed after her.

Even though the place didn't look fancy enough to have cameras in the elevator, I decided to take the stairs up to Sue's fourth floor apartment. On the way, I freshened up by wiping the sweat off my face with the bottom of my t-shirt, slipped on the knit gloves I wore when it first started getting cold, and tucked my braid into my hoodie in the way that Ma hated because combined with my mostly flat chest and baggy clothes, she thought I looked like a boy. On Sue's floor, I spotted her door number from afar, but my feet slowed as I approached.

The hall was empty and I was here, so I told myself to do it. As quickly and silently as possible, I tiptoed to Sue's door, slid the key in the lock and let myself in.

I was standing in the living room. I stayed standing there, waiting for a siren to sound or an attack dog to pounce, but nothing happened. The quiet, homey living room, stayed quiet. It had the usual living room stuff: a couch, an armchair with a blanket that looked like it might be homemade, a small TV and a coffee table. It also had not usual living room stuff in the form of kid's art projects everywhere. There were painted food jar vases holding fake flowers, framed drawings, unidentifiable clay sculptures, and then some. From the looks of it, Sue kept everything any kid ever gave her.

I moved into the living room to get a closer look through the shelves there and felt frustration build. There was so much stuff here and I had no idea what I was looking for, or where it would be. Plus, it felt wrong to look through someone's stuff. I'd already kicked the woman after she was dead, now I was going through her stuff?

I took a deep breath. I was already here. I would be careful and I would be respectful and I'd look where I thought Sue might have left something to do with Michael and that was it. Then I'd leave. So where did someone keep almost 20-year-old information on a baby placement? As far as I knew, they didn't. But I still tried, going through the living room, then the bedroom, closets and even boxes, hoping maybe I'd find a hard drive with old information. I realized I hadn't seen a computer. If Sue had one, it was likely the police had taken it with them... among other things.

Past the living room and connected to the kitchen was a small room that I figured would have been just big enough for one of those cutesy two people cafe tables. Sue had a small writing desk pushed against the wall there instead. The board above the desk was tacked full of papers, some aged and some new. They were notes and letters from kids. Some of them were really sweet, like the one that was obviously a little kid drawing that used circles and triangles and lines to make two people labelled Sue and Kelly holding hands. It was the other kind that drew my attention more. Like the scrawled note that said, "You said you'd make it so I could live with Sean, but you didn't. Don't bother trying anymore. I don't want your help." It was signed Sebastian and the note had creases like it had been folded at one point, and rumples in spots like tears had fallen and dried on it.

I ruffled through the papers and files on her desk, wondering why Sue would keep such a horrible note. She didn't have any files on kids in the system, so either she didn't bring her work home or the police took it back to the city's child services office to be given to someone else. I pulled open the single long, narrow desk drawer. In addition to stationary and pens and tape and stuff, she had blank cards that said, "You matter to me" on the front, and bookmarks with the words

"We all make mistakes sometimes. It's okay to try again."

I looked from the bookmark to the angry note and realized Sue wasn't a masochist. She was just willing to admit her mistakes so she could improve. My fingers reached toward one of the bookmarks. I took in a shaky breath and clenched my fingers closed. I was supposed to be helping Michael, not–

A crash made me jump. My hand shot out and knocked over a glass jar holding pens and pencils in the process. It took a few seconds for fear to recede and my brain function to return and tell me the sound was from outside. Then it informed me someone might have heard the sound of the jar falling over and the writing instruments scattering across Sue's desk. I waited, breath caught in my chest as regular apartment sounds filled the space between my ears: water running in the apartment above. A kid laughing somewhere. Someone singing along with The Weeknd.

I took a deep breath. It didn't help. I hadn't helped anything but I'd done enough. I couldn't stay here any longer. I scrambled to right the glass jar with rainbow coloured tissue paper squares glued on the inside, giving it a stained-glass confetti look. I righted the pens and pencils, and with a longing look at the bookmarks, I closed the desk drawer.

Sue seemed amazing, I could almost convince myself it was okay to take a bit of her kindness with me. But I couldn't, not even a bookmark. I was already disrespecting her by going through her stuff. Now that I knew more about her, doing this was so much harder. Sue could admit her mistakes and learn from them, and I couldn't even figure out what was a mistake and what wasn't. Helping Michael had felt right, but going through Sue's stuff felt so wrong.

I was about to step away from the desk when I noticed something I'd missed. I picked up an inch-long piece of dark wood, bringing it up to my eyes for a closer look. From what I could tell it was a wooden snake miniature that had broken in half. Wondering what significance that had to Sue, I dropped it back in the rainbow coloured pen holder. My gaze flicked up to Sebastian's angry letter. Maybe he gave it to her.

I'd left everything exactly as I'd found it as I searched, so I went straight to Sue's door and peeked out the peephole. No one directly in front of the door. I listened in absolute stillness for a few moments before peeling the door open and peering around. Seeing no one in close vicinity I popped out, locked the door and turned to see the elevator doors open. A crabby looking old man stepped out.

His eyes narrowed the moment he saw me. My blood froze. Had he seen me put a key in Sue's door?

"You one of Sue's kids?"

By 'Sue's kids' I assumed he meant someone who was in the foster system. But I thought I'd clarify anyway. "What do you mean 'Sue's kids'?"

"She was the social worker across the hall," he nodded toward her door. "She's always had these troublemaker kids coming by here when she's not supposed to."

"Oh."

"One of them was here breaking in last week. He's probably the one that went and killed her."

I remembered what Jamie had said: a neighbour had spotted Michael and called the police. I would bet this was the neighbour.

The man shook his head. "The woman's dead and she's still bringing trouble around here."

I was itching to say something to defend Sue, but I couldn't admit I knew her.

'Who'd you say you're visiting here anyway?"

"My aunt," I said, squeezing by the man with as much space as the narrow hall would allow.

The man's bushy brows curved. "There's no Indian lady living here."

"That's because my aunt is…" I scoured my head for a nationality likely to get a pass with the man while pulling open the door to the stairs, "Swiss. Anyway, I gotta go."

I hustled down the stairs and out of the building. I ran all out and didn't stop until I was back at the Centre. I'd been so rushed to get out away from Sue's building I didn't realize I still had a couple of hours to kill until Abbu got to the Centre to pick me up.

"Asiya?" Vicky looked almost worried seeing me. "I thought you weren't coming today?" Her eyes trailed over the athletic wear I never came to the office in. "And why are you all sweaty?"

"I'm lowering my carbon footprint?" I followed her in.

"Huh, well you're totally late." Vicky led the way to the office. "Normally I'm easy-going as long as the work gets done but what a day not to show up until halfway through your shift."

"What do you mean?"

"With Nate gone, this place is a mess. I mean he's

organized as always. But you know, now that he'll probably be gone for a while, we're all trying to get real work done." She grabbed my hands and squeezed. "So help me God, I'm going to get that gazebo built, and I'm going to do it in time for my wedding in the spring."

"Back up a minute, Vicky. What happened to Nate?"

Vicky looked at me like I was the one who was confusing her. "How could you not have heard about Sue being found in the woods?"

"I heard, but what does that have to do with Nate?"

"Oh, right." Vicky's face cleared up. "You've only been here a few weeks, so I guess you didn't meet her. Sue is, well was, Nate's girlfriend."

15

Em, what are we..." My voice trailed off as my brain tried to compute what I was seeing. Em was standing in front of her locker. Usual. She was waiting for me to go to lunch together. Usual. She was talking to a Mutaweenie. So. Not. Usual.

"Ya-ya." Em glanced from me to Ali and back. She knew exactly who the Mutaweenies were at our school. I'd pointed them out to her as the people we needed to avoid like a tattletaling mafia who had me on their hitlist. "Ali and I were just talking about an assignment in Business."

"Oh," I said, in a way that Em clearly knew meant, 'well are you done yet?'

Ali's Mutaweenieness must have kicked in on my arrival because he backed up a step. "I'll, uh, see you in class, Em."

His eyes flicked to mine briefly. I looked away. No way I

was engaging. It didn't matter that we were in school. With him I had to be totally in *masjid* mode. Even if he instigated, if he told on me, I'd be the one everyone talked about, not him.

Em sighed as we headed toward the caf. "Did you really have to be so weird like that?"

"Umm, yeah," I said, feeling bad for just a moment because Ali seemed more like a clumsy, dopey dude than hard core hater. But still, he was a Mutaweenie. "You know the deal. It's weird."

"Well, maybe Ali's not as Mutaweenie as the rest of those weenies."

He was chatting up Em at school and playing religious police at the *masjid*? "Maybe he's more of a weenie than the rest of them."

"Maybe more weenie isn't a bad thing."

Em and I looked at each other and laughed.

"That is so gross," I said. "Please don't make me think about Mutaweenie-weenie."

"Alright, fine." Em slid into a seat, the two gold bangles Ma gave Em as a thank you for all her help with Afiya's many wedding events and many, many bridezilla moments clanged against the cafeteria table. "Anyway, we both know whose weenie you think about."

"Em! I do not." I mean other than that one time. Okay fine God, twice. But You know those were almost totally about biological curiosity and not because I plan to do anything weenie-related.

After a few moments of silence, Em said, "It's been over a week since anyone's seen him."

"Yeah." I hedged.

"Are you alright, Ya-ya? I'm sure he'll be okay."

I didn't know if I believed that. Michael was so desperate to find his parents I was worried what else he'd do. And how long he could keep from getting caught.

I'd tried to help, but Sue's apartment had been a dead end. The only person I knew who knew her was Nate, but…

"Em, you know how that woman who was found dead near where I volunteer?"

"Yeah, that's creepy." Em shuddered.

"Yeah." I shoved images of Sue in the woods somewhere way in the back of my mind. "So it turns out she was Nate's girlfriend. Vicky, the assistant manager, said Nate's so torn up, he just stopped coming to work."

"Poor guy." Em pouted. "He lost the love of his life."

"Yeah, so I was thinking I should go see him," I said. "Just to make sure he's okay."

"Really?" Em asked. "I mean, I'm totally up for operation-sneak-you-out, but you're willing to do this to see your boss – who you said was a pain in the ass – but you weren't willing to try it to see Michael?"

This *was* for Michael.

"Nate is a pain in the ass. That's why he'll probably have no one visiting him." I realized that might actually be true. "Let's just try this one, and we'll see how things go when Michael gets back."

"Alright. We'll start with this." Em's lips curved into a cheeky smile. "And then we'll see about getting you some Michael-weenie."

16

I buzzed from the ground floor of Nate's condo.

"Yesh?"

"Uh, Nate? It's Asiya."

"Unh?" He asked. "You're not ayowed out."

I shrugged before remembering he couldn't see. "I snuck out."

The door buzzed open.

Nate's apartment door opened as soon as I got off the elevator. "Your mother will be maaad." He nodded as if in appreciation, but the effort seemed to make him dizzy and he leaned himself against the door jamb. That's when I noticed he'd been speaking slower and slurrier words than usual.

I peered at him closely. His sweats were sloppy like he'd been wearing them a few days too long, his face was haggard and his eyes were red and glassy looking. If I was guessing correctly, he was drunk.

"I'm drunk." Nate confirmed before pushing himself away from the door and into his apartment.

I'd never seen a drunk person up close – other than people wandering on the street when we went to Toronto to visit Afiya. I'd never gotten a close look cause Ma would clamp a hand on my elbow and drag me away. I followed Nate into his apartment to find him on his couch, head tilted back and mouth open trying to get the last drops out of an obviously empty can of beer.

He looked from the can to me. "Ish empty."

I shook my head and had to bite my lip from smiling when I saw the coffee table. Even Nate's drunken "mess" had his beer cans lined up (and mostly straight) with the tabs popped off in a neat pile in the corner. I picked up the only other thing on the table, a framed picture of Sue and Nate.

I'd never seen him smile so big. Now that I thought about it, I'd never seen Commander Green happy. And Sue, she looked so different. Not just alive, but full of life. One of those people who had a lifetime of kindness confirmed through the smile lines on her face.

"That wush her favourite picture of us," Nate said. "I took it from her apartment, after... after..." Nate shook his head, unable to finish.

I put the frame down carefully. "Do you have someone to help you through this?"

"Patti," Nate said. "But Patti got angry I didn't impregnate Shue, sho I told her not to come."

"Alright." The dealing with a drunk thing was getting less

amusing. "I'll be right back." I went to his kitchen, which of course had Nate's picky perfectionism written all over it. I put some coffee on and filled a glass of water. I didn't have a lot of time and I needed to get him sobered up soon. TV taught me this was how.

I came back with the water and handed it to him.

He just looked at it.

"You need to drink."

"Ish all I've been doing," he said.

"I meant water."

He stared at the water in his hand and then drank.

I sat down on the armchair. "Nate, I'm sorry about Sue."

"Sue wush the best," Nate said, resting his glass on his knee. "There wush no one better than Sue."

"I've heard great things about her."

"She wush great. The best," Nate said. "She wanted to move in together. With me. She wanted to marry me. Know what I shaid? That we had forever to do that shtuff. That we had to focush on foresht, on deforeshtation now." Nate's face crumpled. "Shue wush the best and I loved her and now she's gone."

"Nate." I took the water from his hand before he spilled it. "I know you regret not doing more with her, but she chose you. She wanted a life with you. That has to mean that for the time she was here, *you* made her happy."

Nate turned to me, serious and alert despite the glossy look in his eyes. "I did?"

"You must have, if she wanted more of whatever she had with you."

Nate seemed to be thinking about that, so I took the time to gather the stuff on his coffee table and take it into the kitchen. Then, because I was my mother's daughter, I scraped the plates into Nate's compost, tossed the cans and bottles in the recycling and loaded his energy efficient dishwasher. I came back with Nate's coffee.

He sipped at it silently for a few minutes. "I shoo have been there for her."

"You were."

"Not when she shaw that boy."

I stilled. "What boy?"

"The one who... He did thish to her. The kid the poleesh are searching for." His red rimmed-eyes filled with guilt. "The kid Shue was scared to talk to."

I wanted to cover my ears. My chest thudded. "Sue was scared of him? She told you that?"

"Not at firsht," Nate said. "She liked this one. Shaid that she wanted to help him. That he wush the kind of kid a parent should be proud of. But he wush desperate to know who his birth parents were and she shaid telling him that would hurt him more than help him."

I inhaled a slow breath before asking. "Did she say who Michael's parents are?"

Nate blinked multiple times. Some of the glassiness in his eyes had faded "How do you know hish name?"

"I...He goes to my school."

Nate shook his head, trying to clear it. "Why did you shtop by again?"

"I... wanted to talk to you."

"You snuck out behind your parentsh back, you wanted to talk to me so bad?" Nate asked, leaning forward, then putting out a hand to stop himself from going too far forward.

I shuffled back, but Nate persisted. "Why, Ashi –Asiya?"

"Because I don't think Michael killed Sue."

Nate stood, his lips tight. "I think it'sh time for you to leave."

"He cared about her," I said, standing too.

"Asiya," he said. "Don't make me call your parentsh to get you."

"Okay, fine, I'm going." I stepped to the front door, but stopped to turn back to him. "I am sorry Nate."

"I don't need you to be shorry." Nate dropped back on the couch. "What I need for you to be is gone."

17

The boys and girls mixing leads to fornication," Imam Alwanee's voice boomed through the speaker system. "The problem and challenge for us is that the people in this society think that fornication is a very normal thing to do."

"Oh, look. It's Alweenie's favourite topic," Firdous said.

Alweenie's and Ma's.

Firdous settled her butt further into the masjid carpet, dropped an elbow on her leg, and rested her jaw on her palm. "This should be good."

Leyan leaned across me, so Firdous could hear. "Do you think he's horny?"

I bit my lip hard to stop from laughing but couldn't get control of my shoulders. Ever so slowly, I peered back to see if Ma noticed.

She didn't bother lifting a finger to signal me to shut up.

She just gave me that bulgy-eyed look of hers that said cease and desist all possible unapproved behaviour for the rest of your life, or else.

"You see, being in the presence of the opposite sex presents unnecessary temptation." Alwanee said.

Firdous edged closer. "He's definitely horny. He must wear out his socks crazy quickly."

My teeth clamped so hard on my bottom lip, I thought I tasted blood. I couldn't even open my mouth to tell them to stop because I knew I'd start laughing. I refused to look back.

So, no matter how badly I wanted to, I didn't react when Leyan said, "Okay, so I know he's annoying and horrible and he looks like a lumberjack on Rogaine, but if he weren't completely backwards, he scaled the beard back a bit, and put on some decent clothes, he might have a little something going for him?"

That thought was grosser than Alweenie's laundry.

Firdous came back with, "Stop trying to turn Alweenie into a Mipster." She glared at him with her lip curled. "There's no gentrifying that."

I could hear women behind us whispering. Any minute now Nasreen Aunty would take it on herself to shush us so loudly that even some of the men would turn back to see what was happening.

Instead of Nasreen Aunty, I heard a male voice behind me. One whose words sent a chill through my spine.

"There's the little liar."

My neck twisted even though I willed it not to. Because even though I knew I wouldn't like what I saw, I couldn't not check to see if it was real.

It was. Constable Keith glared at me from the women's entrance to the prayer hall. He pointed a finger at me, turned his wrist over and crooked a finger.

I couldn't.

Keith's eyes narrowed.

I wasn't trying to be defiant. I was paralyzed. Numb to everything except Imam Alwanee's voice, which suddenly seemed super-loud through the speakers but also hard to hear with all the whispering the women were doing and my heartbeat pounding in my ears.

Alwanee paused in his speech. "Can the women please pay attention?"

"That's it." Constable Keith kicked off a shoe.

"Keith, wait," Jamie said.

I hadn't noticed her behind him. A sense of relief flooded me, knowing she was here.

Short-lived relief, since Keith was past listening, even to her. He kicked off his other shoe.

"Either she'll come with us willingly, or I'll arrest her and take her in." As he approached, it was clear he was hoping for the second.

The moment Keith's foot touched the carpet, Nasreen Aunty yelled. "*Ya Allah!* There's a man in the women's section!"

Undeterred, Keith charged toward me, the women along the way scattering a path for him. Some shrieked. Others glued their eyes to the drama to recount in detail. Ma stared at the scene in disbelieving horror.

My gaze darted to where the men were sitting to look

for Abbu. Some of the men were watching. The Mutaweenies looked like their necks would snap with the effort they were making not to. Imam Alwanee yelled from the front, his mic cord trailing behind him as he pushed forward. "What's happening there?"

"Keith!" Jamie yelled, kicking off her own shoes. "If you don't get out of the women's area I'll recommend they pull you off the force until you're spouting community relations out your ears."

That had Keith pause. His piercing gaze darted from me to Jamie and back. Finally, looking like a lion who'd had his prey thwarted, he reversed his course, muttering, "Goddamn sensitivity training," and tromped back to the tile flooring.

I tried to gather the strength to stand, but before I could, Ma rushed over to Constable Keith. He towered almost a foot and a half over her but she clamped her hand on her waist, tilted her head back and gave him her bulgiest bulgy-eye glare. "Why do you bother my daughter like this?"

"Because your daughter lied to me about her boyfriend."

Women gasped.

"Whoa." Firdous whispered beside me. "You're the last one out of us I expected that from."

Oh God. He'd said the b-word. At the masjid. About me. There would be no recovering from this. People would brand me as a Godless hoochie and judge my parents for raising me so loosely. Ma would hate me for as long as they remembered, which would be forever, because if there was one thing Muslims got all root-of-all-evil-in-society about, it was female promiscuity. I looked longingly at a woman in a full burkha and niqab, wishing I could crawl under there and hang out with her a while. At least with her, I could imagine there was a cool, open-minded person underneath instead of the obvious disappointment/shame/disgust/embarrassment for my mother that everyone else displayed. Ma would never forgive me. Oh God, I couldn't breathe.

Imam Alwanee, who'd arrived just in time to hear Keith, proclaimed into his mic, "This." He tsked at me and shook his head at Ma. "Is why girls should not be left alone with the boys."

"My daughter does not talk to boys." Ma scolded Alweenie and Keith. I could hear the usual concrete in her voice crumbling.

"Nice try," Keith muttered, "but I've already heard that one."

"What is this about?" Abbu's voice joined the conversation. My legs finally figured out how to work just enough to take a few wobbly steps to his side.

Jamie cleared her throat. "This is a discussion that we should have back at the police station."

"Why would Asiya need to go to the police station?" Abbu looked to me for answers.

"Because," Keith glared at me. "I have a witness who confirmed sweet little Asiya here went for a romantic stroll in the woods with Michael Riley last Saturday. The same day Sue Desmond's body was found there."

A hush fell over the masjid. By this point, even the Mutaweenies had given up trying not to stare. Every pair of eyes in the masjid landed on me.

Everything but the air pushing through the vents stood still.

Everyone, except Adil.

He jumped out of nowhere. "Abbu, you can't let these pigs arrest Apa!"

Keith sucked in a breath that seemed to make him grow infinitely bigger and rage-ier. "What did you call me?"

"Nothing," I said, finally finding my voice. I rushed to tug Adil behind me and gave him a shove toward the men's side. "He didn't say anything."

Keith's eyes followed Adil.

I stepped forward, cutting off his line of vision. "You wanted to talk to me." I dry-gulped and croaked out the words, "let's go."

"You will not arrest Asiya?" Ma asked Jamie, her voice a tearful plea.

Jamie looked around the congregation, everyone intently listening for her answer. "I think its best we talk at the station."

18

Sitting in a room with Jamie, Keith, and Abbu, I couldn't help but be aware. Aware of how the tiny room was just big enough to fit the table, the folding chairs and the four of us. Aware of how there was no mirror like on TV, but that along the narrow hallway on the way here, we'd passed a room with screens and recording equipment before entering this one. Aware of Keith's rage and Jamie's intent to get the truth this time. Aware that Abbu sat stock still and refused to look at me.

Now that I was here, I didn't know what else I had expected to happen. Of course, the police would question Nate. He was Sue's boyfriend and the director at the Conservation Centre near where she was found. Of course, he told them I'd been in the woods that day.

"You expect us to believe you tripped over a dead body,

said and did nothing. And left your boyfriend to deal with it."

"He's not my boyfriend!"

Keith smirked and nodded knowingly. "So, the rest of it is true."

"I…" I looked over to Abbu who still wouldn't look at me.

"She already told you it's not," Abbu said. "Many times." He'd sat with me through the entire questioning. I'd told him and Ma an abbreviated version in the car. His face had fallen when I said I'd been in the woods with Michael and become unreadable when I said I'd lied to the police about finding Sue. "She told you everything she knows," Abbu said, looking at his watch. "It's almost midnight, now. This is enough."

"She could have done it earlier and under much nicer circumstances but she chose not to," Keith said to Abbu and then leaned his long torso across the table to get in my face. "I'm starting to think maybe he was protecting you from something more than mommy and daddy finding out."

I reached a hand up to grip my pounding head and found the hijab I'd put on before entering the masjid still on. I let my hand fall and turned to Abbu in shock. Was Keith seriously considering *me* a murder suspect?

"That's it." Abbu's chair slammed back. "If you want to ask any more questions, you'll wait for a lawyer."

"I don't have anything else to say. I promise you we just went for a walk," I said it looking at Jamie but meant it as much for Abbu as her. "And not that you asked, but the only reason Michael took Sue's key was because he was looking for information on his birth parents. Neither of us have anything to do with Sue's murder!"

Jamie shot out of her chair. Her face was pallid with anger. I recoiled in my chair, thinking it was directed at me. Then she swung open the door and ground out, "Keith. A word."

As soon as the door closed behind them, I spun to Abbu. "I'm so sorry I lied to you. I didn't—"

"Not now."

"But Abbu, in the woods. I didn't do anything with—"

"I said *not now.*"

I sat there, with Abbu's quiet anger and disappointment radiating through the tiny room. As much as I hated it in here, my stomach was queasy at the thought of what came after. Sweat gathered behind my knees and at the back of my neck. For a moment, I considered taking off the hijab to get some much-needed air, but then I thought it couldn't hurt to keep it on... to remind Ma that I did try to make her happy *most* of the time. Or maybe it would make it worse that I was being questioned at the police station with a hijab on. Like, because I was wearing one, my actions made all Muslims look bad. I was too exhausted to figure it out.

Jamie entered the room alone.

Abbu stood, ready to leave.

I scrambled to follow.

"You said this would be quick." Abbu accused Jamie. "That Asiya would give her statement and we'd go. I trusted you and this is what you do? Accuse Asiya of murder?"

"I'm sorry, Shahid," Jamie said. "I didn't know he'd do that."

Abbu didn't look like he believed her, and neither did I. We watched TV, we knew the routine.

"Keith is a patrol officer who requested to help with this

case." Jamie insisted. "With our limited resources, I couldn't say no."

"I want him away from Asiya," Abbu said.

"He will be," Jamie said. "I'm hoping this will be the last I see of you here, Asiya, but anything you need to talk about, you talk to me, understand?"

I nodded.

"And I'm glad I talked you out of calling a lawyer, because otherwise I wouldn't have had the opportunity to tell you this." Jamie took a slow breath. "Asiya, did Michael ever tell you about his life in Toronto?"

Something gave me the impression I didn't want to hear what Jamie wanted to say.

"A little bit." I glanced at Abbu before adding. "He told me he broke into his social worker's car to get his file."

"That's it?" Jamie asked.

"Is there more?" I asked. My chest was already so heavy I could barely draw breath. Dread fought its way further, filling any little crevice I might have used for air.

"Robbery is the least of it." Jamie closed her eyes briefly, looking truly pained. "I'm risking my career telling you this, but Asiya, you need to understand something about Michael. He's very good at convincing people what he wants them to see."

"What do you mean?"

"I mean he's a good student, right?"

I nodded.

"He's nice, kind, your friend?"

I kept nodding, pausing before agreeing to the last.

"He was also charged with Battery and Assault."

The tiny room closed in on me for a moment before space and air came back to me. I shook my head, sputtering, "I… he… how…"

"He beat a kid senseless. It was so bad the boy had to be hospitalized."

I pressed my fingertips over my eyes and just concentrated on breathing. I stopped trying to think of why, what reason he could have had, how I could make sense of this with what I knew about him. It was too much. I was too tired. I couldn't process anymore.

Still, I had to ask.

"Did he make it all up?" I stole a quick glance at Abbu. "Everything he told me about being a foster child? Was that a lie?"

Jamie shook her head. She'd given up her ever-present professionalism and openly sympathized with my pain. "He was." She swallowed, seeming to erase all lingering emotion and replacing it with resolve. "Kids who go through that, don't always have the best impulse control."

I wished I had that same ability to pull it together because my chin was shaking, and I could barely get my words out. "Are you saying that he… do you think he killed Sue?"

I couldn't meet her eyes as I waited, feeling each moment that Jamie watched me.

"We are closing in on an arrest," Jamie finally said. "And Michael is not the suspect."

Air I hadn't known I'd been holding escaped me.

Jamie noticed. "That doesn't mean Michael is the right

friend for a girl like you."

I'd been about to nod, but stopped at the words 'a girl like you.' Even here, after being caught at the masjid and held at the police station to be told exactly how stupid I'd been, I resented being reminded of how naïve I was.

"I know your experience with boys is limited. And I'm sure he was charming," Jamie said. "No one is blaming you for falling prey to it."

Oh, there would be plenty of blame. And it would start the second I walked out of here. Jamie knew my parents. She should have known better.

"I'm risking a lot telling you all this," Jamie said to Abbu before capturing my gaze. "But I want you to understand once and for all, this is no joke. Whatever Michael is involved in, you do not want to be a part of it."

19

Jamie led us out to the front where Adil leaned, half-sleeping against Ma. Ma sat tightly, her eyes wide and roving with hypervigilance. She nudged Adil as soon as she spotted us.

"Apa!" Adil jumped out of his seat. "Did those pigs try to rough you up?"

A number of police officers stopped what they were doing and turned narrowed eyes in our direction.

"Adil!" Abbu grabbed him by the arm and hauled him out the front doors. The four of us plodded to the car in silence. Abbu dragged Adil ahead and Ma stayed stiffly beside me. The disgust she had for me was clear on her face, so I figured the proximity had more to do with my absolute lack of freedom from here on out. As soon as the car doors shut, Ma whipped around to demand from Abbu, "What has happened?"

I sat with my heart pounding and my arms wrapped

around my waist, trying to hold myself together as Abbu drove, quietly filling Ma in. When he was finished, they were both oddly silent.

I didn't dare try to fill it. I'd never been in trouble on this level. I didn't know what they would do and not knowing was excruciating.

Adil, on the other hand, had a lot to say. "*Apa*, I went to the washroom and on the way I heard this old porker cop say to that stupid piglet that came to the masjid, 'Poor rookie, having a hard time getting info out of a 17-year-old girl?'

"And then the piglet said, 'Screw you. She lied to me.'"

Oh God. Adil didn't get even the best signals in daylight while facing me. There was no way I could signal him to shut-up without alerting my parents. And I was too scared to say or do anything for fear of the torrent that would unleash at the sound of my voice. Unable to do anything but wait, I tried to curl into as small a space as possible as Adil went on.

"And then the porker pig said, 'Aww, and all the rest of the perps coming through here always tell the truth.' Apa, you should have seen how pissed off the piglet was."

I'd made Keith look bad. After embarrassing me in front of my English class and then the entire masjid, it was a pinprick of brightness in my misery. Worry immediately shadowed even that bit of light. Having a cop for an enemy did not seem like a good thing.

"You showed those mofos, Apa."

Except to Adil.

I glanced into the rear-view mirror. Abbu's face was taut and his eyes were on the road ahead of him. Either he wasn't up to date enough to know what a mofo was, or he was so angry at me, Adil got a free pass. Beside him, Ma vibrated with restrained anger.

As we got closer to home, a looming ball of knotted panic densified and made a slow descent down my torso as Abbu turned the car onto our street.

He parked and we all got out, still silent. My parents with anger, me stifled by dread.

"And the coolest thing," Adil continued. "You got out without doing time! I can't wait to tell everyone at school–"

"You will tell no one!" Ma's voice reverberated through the night silence on our street.

"My daughter, alone with a boy. A boy who is in trouble with the police." Ma's voice was so tight and low that it sounded disembodied. "My daughter, taken from the *masjid* to the police station to be questioned about a murder. What will people say, heh? Who can look at such a girl?"

"Ma, I promise we didn't do anything. It was just a walk."

"Walk, talk, did I not tell you to avoid boys? Did I not tell you what will happen?"

"I'm sorry. I–"

"Sorry?" Ma shook with fury. "We let you go to volunteer and you go off with this, this *shadha goonda!*"

I'd been trying to be silent and apologetic to pacify Ma, but I could see her building this into something bigger than it was and getting even angrier by it, so I ever-so-gently clarified. "Ma, Michael isn't a 'white gangster.' Jamie said he–"

The palm that smacked my face landed so fast I didn't see it coming. My lips parted in surprise. My hand raised to my cheek, feeling the rising heat after the sting.

"You are caught lying to the police in front of the entire masjid. Your whole life is ruined because of this boy and you are debating his crimes with me?" Ma blinked back tears like she was the one who'd just got smacked. "Afiya did not give me this kind of trouble. Nasreen's kids do not give her this kind of trouble. What have I done that Allah would give me a daughter such as you, huh?"

Ma's blazing watery eyes settled on Abbu. "I told you she should not volunteer except for the masjid, did I not? I told you she should not be allowed to go alone, did I not? *You* let her go. *You* said we should trust her." Ma glared with everything she had and in the next second her face crumpled. Tears rolled down her cheeks. She fought to stiffen her face. "Now, you deal with *your* daughter."

Ma pushed past Abbu and rushed, sobbing, into the house.

I trembled in frustrated silence. I didn't ask Michael to meet me. I didn't even continue the walk once I knew why he was there. But did she let me explain that? No. There was only room for her rules. Her anger. Her disappointment. And of course, her tears, which would only make what was coming so much worse.

Abbu stared after her. "Adil, go check on your Ma."

Adil, for once getting the hint to stay silent, gave me a pitying look before warily complying.

Standing in the driveway, my hand to my face, I kept a wary eye on Abbu's stiff back. He'd been holding it in since the police station. Since the drive there, really. Just because he was better at keeping himself in check, didn't mean he wasn't as angry as Ma. Angrier, if the amount of time he was taking to decide what to do was any indication.

"You let me down." Abbu whirled around. "You lied. You broke my trust. You embarrassed your Ma in front of the entire masjid. And for what? A boy who dragged you into trouble with the police? Is this the life you want?"

"No! Abbu, I swear I didn't plan to meet him." I pleaded for him to believe me. "And then I thought he–"

"You thought this boy was more important than your family. You lied to us. You lied to the police. And look where it got you." Abbu stalked to the front door. "Your Ma and I raised you better than this."

I followed him up the walk, but stopped short of stepping onto the porch.

"We don't deserve to be coming home from the police station past midnight after barely keeping our daughter out of jail." Abbu said tiredly.

From this height difference, it felt like I was a child again. I stared up at the man who held my safety and happiness way up where he was. A stupidly delusional part of me wished that like when I'd been a child and made choices that had Ma flipping out on me, Abbu would comfort me.

He didn't say a thing. Just stared down at me like he was so unbelievably disappointed. As if he was finally seeing me and didn't like who I was.

My eyes watered. I didn't know what to say to make him understand. "Abbu, I am so sorry. I really didn't–"

"That kind of sorry doesn't fix it." He snapped. "Starting tomorrow you will show how sorry you are by respecting your parents."

His anger faded and his Abbu voice came back. The one he used to talk to me like a person. "I trusted you. I stood up for you and you took advantage of that." Hurt seeped past his anger, before melding with it to make a tone colder and more indifferent than anything I'd ever heard from him. "From now on you will do everything your Ma wishes. And I will not get in her way."

20

School started to feel like a prison. Instead of being grateful for the daily trip away from studying in my room and getting scalding you-ruined-my-life glares from Ma, the realization that these halls and walls would contain the most of my freedom for the foreseeable future, made them feel smaller.

My feet paused in their measured pace as my eyes fell on a specific locker. Michael's. We'd set up some possible times for me to meet him behind the plaza. To tell him what I'd found. Yeah right, I was going to go tell him what I'd found out.

Anyway, he already knew what it had taken me getting dragged to a police station to understand: I was an idiot. Book-smart, maybe, but when it came to life I was hopelessly naïve.

Everything that happened with Ma was expected. Her love was conditional and she never pretended otherwise. Sure, it sliced me every time I realized it, but her slap in the face was a papercut compared to Michael's betrayal. He'd worked hard to make me think that he saw who I was, that he actually cared. Stupid me.

"Ya-ya!" Em fell into step with me, hooked a friendly arm around mine and yanked me to a stop. "Why haven't you been returning my calls?"

"A lot has been going on." I wished could unload, but there wasn't enough time to get into it between classes.

"Uh, yeah. What happened at the police station?" Em cleared her throat. "And after."

I'd forgotten Em had gotten to know Firdous and Leyan through Afiya's multiple wedding events. They must have filled her in.

With Em's long black duster buttoned closed, it reminded me of an *abaya* again. Reminded me of wanting cover at the masjid and finding none. "It wasn't good," I said, frustration, grief and anger flooding my voice till it cracked.

"Aww, sweetie." Em squeezed me in a sidehug. "Just say the word and we'll run away together."

I was about to take her up on the offer, but the final bell for the period cut into even a moment of imaginary freedom.

"I've got to go." I pulled away. I didn't want to be even a bit late in case the attendance went down to the office without me and Ma got a call home. I yelled over my shoulder as I hustled to class. "I'll fill you in at lunch."

I rushed to Mrs. Lee's Chemistry class and opened the door, ready to tiptoe in as quietly as possible when I realized that for once, the class wasn't absolutely silent as soon as the bell rang. In fact, they were not only talking, most had their phones out. So did Mrs. Lee.

A couple people saw me come in and stared as if I had something interesting to say. Others noticed. Slowly the buzz in the room settled down.

"You work with him, right?" Eileen asked me.

"Um, who?" I cautiously made my way to my desk. I eyed Mrs. Lee, wondering if she was okay with this conversation carrying across the class. She seemed as interested in my answer as everyone else.

"That Nate guy."

"Yeah." I stopped at my desk. "I do my volunteer hours with him at the Sheriden Conservation Centre. Why?"

"She doesn't know," someone behind me said.

My pulse quickened. My phone was solely for the purpose of Ma getting in touch with me, so I had no data. "What happened?"

"Nate Wagner was arrested today," Mrs. Lee said, "for murdering his girlfriend."

21

Tuesday went by as another day of my new penitentiary normal went by before school socked me with another surprise on Wednesday.

Michael.

I'd heard he was back before I saw him. As soon as I entered the school, actually. Michael was here and everybody was talking about it.

I saw him between first and second period. A crowd in the hallway swelled around him. The same people who'd doubted him, *his friends*, were welcoming him back like he was a long lost king. I stared from a distance, practically hearing him in my head. *Help me Asiya, please. I can see that you want to.*

Yeah, because of all the stupid people fawning over you, I was the stupidest.

I stalked off, wondering why I'd bothered stopping. The

best thing I could do was avoid Michael till graduation. Then he'd be off being a journalist like he'd once told me he wanted to be, or committing robberies and beating up people like he apparently tended to in his spare time. Either way, what he did had nothing to do with me.

I couldn't avoid him in English. He came to talk to me the first chance he got.

"Are you okay?" he asked. He couldn't say more than that. The softness in his face, the concern in his eyes did it for him.

His voice was so sincere, his worry so real, I faltered. Then I remembered. He was a liar – a good one. Michael couldn't possibly care less about me.

"I'm fine," I said, making sure to say nothing more with my face or voice. Then I got up and walked over to talk to someone else.

I managed to lose him right after class and dodge him all day. It was exhausting, always being vigilant. But I had to keep it up. He knew I was avoiding him now. Hopefully he'd take the hint and give it up.

On the way home, I decided to do something about the other thing that had been bothering me all day. I pulled out my phone and made a call.

"Vicky, did you hear?" I figured it was fine to call the Centre from my cell. If Ma or Abbu asked why, I could say I needed to tell someone I wasn't coming back.

"Uh, yeah," Vicky said. "The police were all over this place. They found this creepy looking statue thing with a missing dick on his shelf."

"What?" I asked, trying hard to follow.

"Yeah," Vicky went on. "I heard one of them say he probably kept it like a trophy. The statue, not the dick." She paused. "Although what he did with the dick is anyone's guess."

"Why would Nate want a… penisless statue for a trophy?"

"It was one of those sick trophies that killers keep to remind them of their victims," Vicky said.

This did not make any sense. Why would Nate use a peni– a statue of any kind to kill his own girlfriend and then display it? "They found it on his shelf?"

"Yup. Right there on display."

After hearing that Nate was dating Sue, I couldn't help but peek into his office. I'd noted how his minimalist discipline was nothing like Sue's homey warmth. His desk had been empty, his shelf sparse. There had been no statue. "It wasn't there last week."

"Well, the police found it there."

"Where?"

"Right next to the globe," Vicky said.

"Where one of the raised fists made of recycled metals was?"

"No, in between the globe and the metal fist."

"Like filling in the empty space?"

"Uh, yeah," Vicky said. "What's with the weird questions? You're starting to sound like Nate or something."

"Exactly! Nate would never fill in that empty space. The lack of balance would throw him in a tizzy."

Vicky laughed uncomfortably. "Look, he's obviously not right in the head, so trying to make sense of him just isn't going to work, is it?"

"Come on Vicky." I finally put into words what I'd been thinking since I'd heard about the arrest. "You don't really think Nate killed someone, do you?"

"Well, the statue was there, so what am I supposed to think?" Vicky asked. "And the police must think it's the murder weapon for a reason."

The RCMP had accused Abbu of being a terrorist for a reason too: they were capable of being idiots, just like everyone else.

Vicky sighed. "Look, this stuff with Nate is out of our hands, so enough about that. But I'm dying here. Do you think you can come in a couple times this week to help out?"

"Umm, Vicky… I have something to tell you."

"Why do I get the feeling I won't like this?"

"I can't volunteer at the Centre anymore."

"God dammit, are you for real?" Vicky didn't hold back her disappointment. "How could you do this to me right now? We need to get going on the gazebo."

"I'm sorry, Vicky I just can't come anymore."

"This is because I told the police about you and that kid walking in the woods, isn't it?"

"You what?"

"I saw you out the window," Vicky said. "What was I supposed to do, lie to the police?"

So, that was how Keith zeroed in on me so easily in English class. He already knew. But then why didn't he do anything about it? He obviously wanted to. Jamie. She'd held him back afterschool and at the police station. She must have been looking out for me the whole time. I owed her so big.

"Look I'm sorry if you got in trouble, but I'm swamped here," Vicky said, not actually sounding very sorry. "I gotta get going, alright? Bye!"

I pulled the phone from my ear and stared at it before pocketing it and turning up my driveway. I faced off with my front door and sighed. If school was prison, home was solitary.

I'd gotten away with a few hours in my room studying before I heard yelling downstairs. Figuring Ma had worked up an anger again and started without me, I went down to see what triggered her to remember how much she detested me this time.

I found her in the kitchen standing over Adil, waving a piece of paper in her hand. "You bring home a 'D' on your math test and instead of telling me, you go down to play video games?"

"It's not a 'D,'" Adil made the mistake of clarifying. "It's a 'D+.'"

"A 'D+!'" Ma's mouth moved as if she tasted something bitter as she caught sight of me. "Even Asiya can manage A's."

As much as Adil's refusal to grow up bothered me sometimes, I hated being used to shame him. Mostly because I hated when Ma used not being as good as Afiya to shame me.

"But Ma, that's not fair." Adil muttered. "I'm not smart like that."

"*Hai!*" Ma tugged at her hair. "You are not smart because you do not try harder."

I felt for Adil. Sure, he could work harder at school. But that didn't mean it would be as easy for him to pull the same grades Afiya and I did.

"What's this?" Abbu's voice joined the conversation. Ma's yelling was so intense I hadn't heard him come in. He took the paper from Ma's hand and gave Adil an incredulous look. "How do you get a 'D' on a math test?"

Grades were the one place where Abbu joined in on the child-shaming. And considering Ma and Abbu were still livid about me, Adil had a tidal wave of hurt coming his way.

"Math is hard early in the year," I said, not knowing which parent to focus on. Ma wasn't in the most rational mood and Abbu still wouldn't look at me. "Different teachers expect different things when showing your work. I'm sure Adil will figure out what his teacher wants now."

"It does not matter how well you show the work when the answers are wrong." Ma snapped. She looked from Adil to me and back, as if not knowing who to be angry at. "No mother in the world has had the kind of trials you two are giving me!"

"I'll help him."

Ma scoffed. "The whole world knows you have forgotten all about your studies."

That wasn't fair. I worked hard at school. I looked to Abbu, but he was staring a little too determinedly at Ma.

Okay fine. Abbu wanted me to make Ma happy. I would.

"Actually," I said carefully. "I was thinking maybe I'd join the Quizbowl team at school this year."

"You think I am stupid, *nah*?" Ma asked. "You are looking for another way to stay with this *goonda* of yours."

I knew better than to clarify about gangsters this time.

"What if I asked Principal Wootten if I could join the team but practice on my own?" The team didn't do so well last year. He'd all but offered to work around Ma's limitations for me. I knew he would bend over backwards at the chance to have a winning team.

Ma stared at me with narrowed eyes as she searched for my nefarious angle.

"They talk about the Quizbowl in the Sheriden Observer," I said, offering it on a platter. "Sometimes the winners make the front cover."

That had Ma's pupils flare momentarily before she returned to eyeing me with her recently customary disdain. "We will see how you do."

I reached over to squeeze Adil's arm. This was as much of an opening as we were going to get. It was time for us to make a getaway. "We'll go start on Adil's math right now."

"I'm sorry my crap is making things harder for you," I said, once we were in my room with the door shut.

"That's okay Apa," Adil said. "And thanks for defending me to Ma and Abbu." He reached up to hook an arm around my neck, a smile breaking out on his face. "Sometimes I get frustrated with you being so perfect, but then you're all awesome and I forgive you."

Umm, okay. "I'm not perfect," I said.

"Sure you are," Adil said.

"I think you're confusing me with Afiya."

"Nope." Adil shook his head. "Afiya Apa's beyond perfect. She's overkill."

I laughed. She totally was. Adil and I looked out for each other as much as we could. Afiya looked for ways to look better in front of our parents, even if it meant using one of us as the footstool up to her pedestal.

"Still." I insisted. "I'm nothing close to perfect. Have you not been paying any attention to all the trouble I've gotten into lately?"

"Exactly," Adil said. "You can do all that school and grades stuff Afiya Apa does, but you've got other skills."

I laughed. "Like what, flipping roti with Ma?"

"Like standing up to that cop for Ma and me, or covering for that Michael guy," Adil said. "When someone needs your help, you're pretty badass."

I took in a staggered breath. I didn't actually believe what Adil was saying, but I wanted to. I wanted to be the kind of person that would stay and help when things got hard, instead of just caring when people met stupid conditions. I wanted to be badass.

"I pay attention." Adil tapped his head proudly. "I'm not stupid when books aren't involved."

"You're not stupid, period," I said. I needed to change the subject. I couldn't process the direction my head was going with Adil here. I mean, how did you get to seeing someone in jail? I shook off the thought and turned to Adil. "Now let's see if you can pay attention to math."

"What? We're really doing that?" Adil frown-pouted. "There's no point. I'm not good at it."

"Don't give up." I nudged him toward my desk. "You're just not good at it yet."

22

I'd spent all morning mentally running through my lunchtime plans. I'd scouted the shortest, least likely to be driven by someone I knew route to Sheriden's jail, researched the visitation process and found a place for a pit stop on the way. Time-wise it was tight, but I was pretty sure I'd make it back for English. I'd better or all my effort this morning to convince Wootten I'd be able to rock the Quizbowl without attending afterschool practices with the team would be a waste. And that wouldn't be the worst of it. I had exactly zero strikes left with Ma.

I had my bag ready and as soon as the lunch bell rang, I was off. I sighted my chosen exit, then kept my eyes two feet ahead of me, finding spaces in the lunchtime crowd and sidling through. I was so intent on making time, I failed to notice a tall figure coming at me. Until I rushed right into him.

"Ow." I grabbed my nose. My hand fell from my face, my snubbed nose forgotten when I saw whose chest I'd bumped into.

Michael's hands grabbed my upper arms. To everyone else it looked like he was steadying me. I knew better. His eyes were hard and when his tight lips moved, they weren't offering an invitation. "We need to talk."

I laughed. "We have nothing more to say."

"Why are you avoiding me?"

"Maybe because I'd rather not be beaten to a bloody pulp too."

Michael's eyes did that thing where within a blink a bunch of emotions played out: confusion, recognition, surprise, anger, regret, frustration – and sadness? – before he settled on determination. I saw it a split second before his hands tightened on me.

"Let me go." I yanked unsuccessfully in his grip. "I don't want to talk to you."

Michael responded by shifting to stand to the side and a bit behind me. I sucked in a surprised breath when his arms wrapped around me in tight hug. In my shock, I moved with him as he navigated the few feet through the crowd to the set of fire doors I'd been trying to reach. I pushed at him, freeing myself of his hold. I walked with him past the stairs, planning to ditch him and get on my way outside. Except instead of exiting the second set of doors Michael hooked a turn, taking me with him into the shadowy area under the stairwell. The space that couples used to hookup during class.

"Seriously?" I asked, shaking off his hand.

"From what I hear, we've already had quite the kiss." Michael shrugged as if none of this mattered. "Apparently I lack finesse."

I crossed my arms, refusing to be embarrassed. I'd lied to Em, my parents, even the police *to help him*. That was nothing compared to the things he hadn't told me.

"But I guess I missed that part," Michael said, his indifference dropping with every word. "Just like I missed the part where you stopped giving a shit about me while I worried like crazy every time you didn't show up."

A pang of guilt and something more zipped through me. I shook it off. I was not falling for this again. "You're back. You have tons of people to keep you company." I moved to pass him. "You don't need to keep up the pretense with me."

Michael planted himself in my way. "You're assuming things about me and you won't give me a chance to explain."

"You assume you deserve one!"

Michael staggered back, as if I'd smacked him so hard I propelled him. Like my words had cut him on a level I hadn't thought of. I looked down. As much as I wanted, *needed*, to get away from him, I didn't want to do it like this. "You wanted to talk," I said, quietly. "Do it quick."

For a moment Michael didn't move, just watched me. Then he slumped back against the wall and slid down to sit with his elbows hanging over his knees. He stared down at his hands before looking up at me. "You think I'm violent. Because of what the police told you."

"Are you telling me you weren't convicted of assaulting that kid?"

Michael's face tightened. "They only told you one side of the story."

I raised an eyebrow and waited.

He took in a deep breath. "Do you remember that day you and Em were cursing Bryant?"

I nodded. That was the day I'd first really noticed Michael. It could go down as the day that began my downfall.

"You asked me how I knew Bryant was such a douchebag. And I told you I knew the type. Because the guy I fought with, he was that type." Michaels mouth twisted like he tasted something bitter. "He knew exactly how to take shots at people and get away with it, just like Bryant knew he'd get away with what he did because he did it off school property.

"The guy, he would come after me and we'd get into it. But then he'd pretend he was the victim, and he had parents who stood up for him, the teachers defended him. Hell, even the principal refused to discipline him for fighting, even though he had no problem coming down on me with detentions and suspensions."

"So you decided to fight hard enough to get arrested instead?" I asked. "How was that supposed to help?"

"It's a whole lot better than sitting around being a victim in my own life."

Michael's words hit a little too close to home, and my face must have shown it because he popped up immediately. "I didn't mean you. Asiya, I–"

"So it was self-defence?" I asked, cutting off the beginning of a conversation that would undoubtedly leave me vulnerable. Trusting Michael wasn't something I could afford to do again.

"That's not how the police made it sound."

"I told you they hate me," Michael said, frustration seeping through every syllable. His eyes pled with me. "Don't let them turn you against me."

I searched his face for the lie. I didn't find anything except pain and loneliness. And an uncomfortably real longing for me to believe him. For all that his emotions seemed true, it also didn't get past me that he didn't confirm or deny anything.

"*You* turned me against you when you lied to me. It should have happened the first time when you lied to me about staying with Sue to call the police, but this time? Not telling me you assaulted somebody?" I shook my head. "What did you expect to happen?"

Michael ran a clenched hand through his hair. "I just wanted a chance to show you who I am aside from that stuff."

"That *stuff* is your life."

"No, that stuff was my circumstance," he said. "My life is what I choose."

Michael looked like he wanted to say more, a lot more. "Asiya, I–"

I shook my head. I could not hear this. "I can't fall for this again."

Michael reached for me at the same time I moved to leave.

I flinched. My eyes zeroed in on the hand that had moved toward my face.

We stood there frozen in place. Background noise from the halls drowned out by the sound of our breaths.

Slowly, Michael's hand lowered. His voice quiet, toneless, he said, "You're not scared of me."

I could have confirmed it, but I stayed quiet.

"You're angry that I didn't tell you. You trusted me. You tried to help me and got burned for it." Michael's body strained with unchecked energy. Like he was dying to move and was forcibly holding himself still. "But you don't believe I'd hurt you."

I knew how he felt. The desire to move tamped down by the need to stay put was horrible.

"You *know* I wouldn't hurt you." Michael's eyes pleaded with me. "You wouldn't have stayed here to talk with me if you believed that."

I did know it, and I was so transparent Michael knew I knew it. I had no reason to believe him, to feel safe with him, to want to be here with him, but I did. "I'm an idiot."

"No." Before I could blink he'd gathered me to him saying things I didn't know I wanted to hear. "You're smart. And caring and so much more courageous than you think."

Within a moment he became the boy from the woods. The secret crush come alive to see me in a way no one other than Em ever had. More, because the way he held me tucked into him, the way he crooned to me telling me how sorry he was for not telling me everything, for getting me in trouble, for getting me involved at all, was so much warmer and affectionate than anything I'd felt in so long.

My heart pounded. My breathing shallowed.

I couldn't do this.

I wrenched out of Michael's arms so abruptly he startled. He watched me, no doubt confused by the real fear on my face.

"I have to go."

"Asiya, don't–"

I should have gone to the cafeteria, sought safety with Em and visited Nate another day. I moved to the doors, breaking free into daylight instead. I needed to run.

23

The reflection in the mirror of the Tim Horton's bathroom I'd stopped at halfway to the police station showed that without a doubt I was my mother's daughter. Even though Ma was a small woman, the big baggy ¾ length cardigan I'd pulled over the *salwar kameez* I was wearing filled me out, making me look older, more like her. The silver mascara I'd applied sparingly to strands of my bangs and the too-pale-for-me face makeup I'd pilfered from Afiya's old room helped age me further. I wrapped my braid into a bun, draped an *urna* over my head, and slid on Abbu's spare reading glasses for good measure.

Reaching into my bag for the driver's licence I'd borrowed from Ma's wallet, I glanced in the mirror. I could pass… except for the child-like innocence in my eyes. I scowled. No wonder everyone wanted to tell me what to do.

I channelled Ma, narrowing my eyes. Hmm, too squinty.

I scrunched my face. That just made me look constipated.

I widened my eyes, bulging them out as much as I could. Ma's 'talk back and I'll incinerate you' look stared back at me. Effective, but a little much to visit someone in jail.

I pinched my lips in a tight reverse pout. Ma's I've-lived-a-thousand-times-longer-than-you-so-just-be-quiet-and-obey-you-insignificant-child face. Perfect!

I'd have to head back to class looking like this. I was on a tight timeline after…after wasting too much time on things that couldn't go anywhere. I needed to get myself into the jail. My feet only got the message as far as the front entrance. Once there, they rooted themselves in the cement, planted in fear.

Alright God, here's the thing. I totally thought You were giving me like a Thou-shalt-have-gastrointestinal-discomfort-until-you-do-the-right-thing wink. Not to offend your Almighty sensibilities or anything, but some of us are slower than others. You gotta be clear about when it's a God Sign and when it's indigestion. Not that I'm blaming You.

The whole Michael thing was my bad. I get it and I'm trying my best to stay away. But this thing with Nate. He's innocent. I know it. And Sue, she was a good person. I know You don't want me to stay silent while an innocent man goes to jail for an injustice against someone like Sue. So I'm going to do this thing, because it's the best I can come up with. And I know You've got a lot, like a lot of people to watch over, but maybe you could spot me on this one?

With that and a quick reminder to myself that since the jail was right next to the police station, I was more likely to get caught by someone who recognized me standing on the outside looking suspicious than I was on the inside trying to see Nate. I unglued my feet and got myself to the person at the front desk. I heard myself ask to see Nate. He asked for ID and I handed over Ma's licence. He went back and forth from it to me.

With my pinched mouth closed, I took level breaths through my nose, which seemed to draw his attention. Damn it, he'd noticed. Ma had a straight small nose that Afiya got. Adil and I took after Abbu's slightly squatter nose.

"I did a much better job contouring that day," I said.

The man looked from the picture on the licence to me, gauging if makeup could make up the difference. He broke into laughter, shaking his head. "You women!"

My heart pounded as I nodded. That was me – one of the many middle-aged women who'd forgotten to cosmetically thin out her nose that morning.

He handed me the licence, had me (Ma) fill out a form and had a guard lead me down a hall. I followed, praying we weren't walking to a cell of my very own. He opened the door to a room. "Wait here."

I guess I'd been expecting a room like the one I'd been interrogated in. This one was bigger, but had a table and glass separating me from the other side. A few excruciating minutes later, a door opened and Nate entered.

Nate's eyes widened as recognition flashed in them. I saw his mouth move. "Asi–"

"Nate." I cut him off quickly, indicating the phone.

Nate took a hint and kept quiet until the officer left us.

"What are you doing here?" Nate asked immediately,

his eyes taking in each detail of my getup. "And who are you supposed to be?"

"My mother." I waved off Nate's shock. "I needed to talk to you. I know that statue wasn't in your office last week."

"Statue?"

"The one the police are saying you used to kill Sue," I said, impatiently. "Do you not know this?"

"I know." Nate's voice trailed. "I just don't understand what it has to do with you."

"I… I want to help you," I said. "Nate, I know you didn't kill Sue."

Nate's eyes filled with pain at the mention of Sue. His lips tightened. "But why come see me?" Nate asked. "Why not just tell the police what you know?"

I looked down, embarrassed. "That day you sent me to take pictures for the Centre? I ran into Michael and we went for a walk in the woods. We found Sue."

"You saw her."

The pain in Nate's red eyes skewered me and the words came burbling out. "We found her body by accident. I ran away and pretended it didn't happen so I wouldn't get in trouble with my parents. I'm sorry. I'm so sorry I left her and I'm sorry I lied to the police about not being there because they found out and now they won't believe anything I say to defend you."

Nate's face turned to stone. "You shouldn't have bothered coming."

"I'm really sorry, Nate. Sue was a good person and she deserved better."

"How would you know that?"

"I, uh, read about her." I felt bad for not coming completely clean, but I was losing him already. I could see it from the rage on his face. "Being a good person didn't save Sue and following the rules hasn't done much for me. I didn't do the right thing then, but I want to now."

"Well maybe I don't want your help."

I swallowed, coming to terms with just how true Michaels words had been. "Things don't change for people who sit around being victims," I said. "I know I'm the last person you'd want to help figure out who really killed Sue, but I'm pretty sure I'm the only person here."

Nate stared at me, unblinking. All at once he turned away. His hand fisted against his mouth as he choked back hard swallows. "I can't believe this. I can't believe Sue's gone. I can't believe they think I killed her." He swallowed, working hard to contain himself before looking back at me. "I can't believe you're my only help."

I tried not to take offense to that. "Do you have a lawyer?"

"Sure. He says it doesn't look good. I was with Sue Saturday morning. I was late getting to work and I was the last one to see her." Nate looked down. "Other than whoever killed her. But she was at home when I left. No one else saw her all morning, and her car was still at home, so they think she came to the woods willingly, with me."

"Why were you late that day?" I asked. "You hate missing your walk."

Nate's eyes seemed to be measuring me. He took his time before answering in the slightest whisper. "I was late because Sue and I argued before I left. The police don't know that part.

I'd rather they not find out."

"Believe me, I'm not planning on chatting with the police any time soon," I said. "Is there anyone you can think of who would want to frame you?"

"One." Nate watched me and then spoke slowly. "I know he's your friend, but this Michael kid. He was really pushing Sue. He was pathological about finding his parents. And he just happened to show up with you for a walk and then you guys stumbled on Sue? He could have led you there, Asiya."

I'd thought about this. "I led the way that day. Michael followed me."

"On a path he could have seen you take in previous weeks."

No. I shook my head. It hadn't been like that. "If Michael didn't have an alibi or something to absolve him of the crime, why would the police have let him go?"

"I don't know," Nate said. "I didn't tell you this when you came to my apartment, but Michael practically harassed Sue to help find his parents."

Michael was determined about finding his parents. I knew this. But he wouldn't have gone after Sue…

"And because Sue hated seeing anyone hurting, she attempted to approach the birth mother."

Michael's mom. She really was in Sheriden.

"The woman wanted nothing to do with him," Nate said. "She was adamant Sue not say anything."

My heart felt like it flipped over and flopped hard in my chest. How could she do that to him. Her own child?

"Sue was devastated. She avoided seeing Michael, because she didn't want to have to tell him he was at a dead end. It's possible she did and he got violent when he didn't receive the information he wanted." Nate blinked. "If she called him after I left, I'm willing to bet she would have written about it in her journal."

"What journal?"

"Sue did most of her venting in a journal."

I didn't remember seeing one at Sue's. "Do the police have it?"

"I don't know." Nate looked down. "I don't think so. If they did and she'd written about us arguing, they'd have their motive and probably wouldn't still be questioning me to find something more. Her journal is probably hidden somewhere in her apartment still."

I swallowed. It would be even harder for me to sneak away now than before. Not to mention, I was trying to sneak back into Sue's apartment after I'd admitted to Jamie I'd done it before and handed over the key. If I got caught this time, I doubt she'd let me off as easily. "How do I get in?"

"Call my mother." Nate recited her number for me to memorize. "Patti can go to my place and get Sue's spare key."

"All right," I said. I checked my watch. I needed to head back. As it was, I'd be late for class. "I should go."

"One thing." Nate cleared his throat. "Don't tell Patti about the statue. She was the one who brought them back for Sue from a trip to the Ivory Coast. Patti hoped giving Sue fertility statues would convince me to," Nate flushed, "to 'stop tree hugging and get on bush patrol.'"

Whoa. A mom who encouraged her kid to have sex, or at least if bush patrol was what I thought it was… Huh. Who knew.

"I heard that the statue was um, that it…"

"That it what?" Nate asked.

"That it was missing uh, it's… penis," I said. "Was it missing? When you saw it last?"

"I don't think so." Nate frowned. "I mean, I didn't look for it, but I don't remember it not being there."

So, it was possible the penis was lost during the murder. I straightened like I'd been zapped. "What did it look like?"

"The penis?"

Yes, the penis, but I couldn't get myself to say that. "The statue."

"It was carved out of a dark wood. Almost charcoal in colour."

A charcoal-coloured wooden penis… I really needed to get back into Sue's.

"I have to go, but Nate, I promise I'll do what I can."

Nate nodded, not looking particularly reassured. "Be careful around him, Asiya."

Pacing my way out of the jail, I felt like nothing had changed: Sue was dead, people thought Michael killed her, and I was in over my head. Despite the lighting and ventilation, the path out of the jail felt heavy to the point of suffocation. The feeling of doom chased me to the front doors. Getting involved hadn't gone well for me the first time around. I could only pray this time would be better. I pushed past the doors.

And collided with someone coming inside.

"Whoa." Constable Sean Keith's hand shot out and grabbed my arm.

24

My heart hopped into my throat and got stuck there. I had only one thought: God and I really must have our signals crossed up again because this totally hadn't been what I meant by "spot me."

And then Keith released me and pulled his face off his phone. I used that moment to turn away and pull the *urna* resting on my head, lower over my face.

"Excuse me, ma'am," Keith said. "I didn't mean to scare you."

I kept my face averted and – since I couldn't be me and a South Asian accent was too close to Ma – I faked an Arab accent. "No *broblem*."

Keeping my head down and my eyes on the steps, I rushed away from the jail. A breeze blew and caught my *urna*. I swiped it back like a cat snatching a fly mid-air as I scurried down the sidewalk.

"Hey!"

Uh-oh.

"Wait!" Footsteps hurried behind me.

It was totally possible Keith was rushing for a perfectly logical reason that didn't concern me. Like a prison break, I thought hopefully and moved to cross the street.

"I said stop!" A hand clamped down on my shoulder and spun me around quite ungently.

"Hey!" I yelled, trying to keep my face averted. "*Zis iz bulice brutality!*"

"You can drop the accent, Asiya." Keith released my arm, but his Satan eyes lasered me to the spot. "What were you doing in there?"

"What, a person can't walk into a public building?"

He cocked an eyebrow. "In a disguise?"

I shrugged innocently. "I can't dress in tribute to the motherland?"

"Which would be what? Arabistan?"

Oh. He'd caught that.

"Yeah. I caught that." Keith read my mind, or more likely my face. He sneered. "Just because I don't care for sensitivity protocol in a mosque when someone lies to me about a murder investigation, doesn't make me an idiot."

"I don't think you're an idiot because of that," I said graciously. I wondered where this antagonism was coming from. Something about Keith – probably the way he humiliated me in front of my entire English class and then with the whole masjid as witness – had me fighting back first and thinking second.

Keith's face flamed. "Keep it up. It'll give me time to think of something to arrest you with."

And just like that, my chest lurched and my throat closed, causing my breath to come out in a strangled squeak.

A satisfied expression practically glowed from Keith's face.

"What for?" Anger released the hold on my throat. "I didn't do anything illegal!"

Not that he knew of. But he was accusing and convicting me anyway. I bristled at the injustice of it.

"Tell me what you're up to," Keith said impatiently, like he was tired of asking it.

Well I was tired of being told what to do. I crossed my arms and waited.

"All I have to do is go back in there and ask around." Keith tilted his head toward the jail.

"I'd love to stick around while you do." I took a tiny test step backward. "But I'm late for class."

"Asiya." A warning stretched loud in that one word.

I raised an eyebrow. "Did you want to write me a note?"

"Tell me what you're up to." Keith growled.

Fine, he wanted to know? "You know you have the wrong guy, right?"

For a second, Keith looked taken aback. Then, he snarled. "What do you know about it?"

There was no point backing down now. "I was at the Conservation Centre last Saturday."

Keith's eyes narrowed on me.

"As a volunteer! I looked in Nate's office and I clearly

remember there was no statue in there."

"That doesn't mean a thing," Keith said. "He could have brought it in any time after that."

"He said he wasn't there."

"How many times do you expect me to fall for that one?"

"If you knew Nate at all, you'd know he'd never leave the statue between the fist and the globe. The lack of balance would drive him nu–"

"How did you know where..." Keith shook his head, getting quiet. For once, I couldn't recognize one of his usual expressions: arrogance, anger, and accusation.

Then he spoke, and from his quiet tone, I realized he was beyond emotion. Keith was about to combust. "From the beginning of this case." He stepped forward, forcing me to back up. "Every single step of the way, all you've been is a pain in my ass."

I took another step back. Keith followed.

"I'm going to find out why you were in there." He shoved his thumb back toward the jail. "And then I'm going to find you." He smiled, a little too happily in my opinion considering the subject. "And this time no one's going to be able to protect you from me. Not daddy, not Jamie, no one."

That's it. I was done with this conversation. I backed up and–

A car honked, and Keith yelled "Watch it!" at the same time.

I caught myself at the curb. Just before I'd almost run right onto a busy road.

"Use the damn crosswalk!" Keith yelled over his shoulder

as he stalked toward the jail. "If jaywalking came with prison time I'd arrest you right now and save myself the trouble."

I watched Keith's back as his legs ate up the ground to the jail doors. It would be minutes before he found out I'd impersonated Ma. How long would it take for him to come after me?

Even though I knew I was screwed on a level where it made no difference, I raced back to school. At least I'd be where Ma expected me to be when Keith arrested me.

25

I slowed as I reached the school, so I could focus on forcing air into my lungs. I was 20 minutes late for class. I had no time to change, no time to get books, and no time to catch my breath.

I lucked out, as a guy in my Grade who I thought might be named Isaac walked by the side door of the school I was standing outside of. I knocked, motioning for him to open it.

He raised an eyebrow and stepped back to let me in. "I didn't know you skipped class."

"I'm just late," I said. Really late.

Isaac nodded and was off to wherever he was going. I jogged in the opposite direction toward class.

I'd almost reached the hallway I needed to turn down when Wootten stepped out from that direction.

His eyes popped open, as wide as mine. Possibly wider.

"Mrs. Haque!" He said. Was that fear in his voice? "What are you…" he squinted. "Asiya? Is that you?"

"Umm, yeah."

"What are you doing out of class?" Wootten placed a hand on his chest as if to calm his chest. "And why are you dressed like your mother?"

"I, um… was getting ready for a presentation." I'd spent the whole run back looking over my shoulder for fear of Constable Keith coming up and tackling me from behind. I hadn't bothered to stop and change.

"I was just in your classroom. The attendance went to the office with you marked absent."

Great, I would get caught committing identity fraud and skipping on the same day.

He frowned. "Asiya, imagine the learning missed while you got ready."

I was about to begin apologizing profusely.

"What if Mr. Mathis covered something you get asked at Quizbowl?" Wootten asked. "How would you feel then for not knowing the answer?"

Seriously? I'd run so hard I had a stitch in my side. I had a big, angry cop gleefully rubbing his palms together as he prepared to arrest me, and Ma was going to be so angry she'd probably leave me in jail and pretend she never had me. My life was about to come to an end, and Wootten wanted me to think about the Quizbowl?

"I don't think I can be in the Quizbowl anymore."

"What?" Wootten gasped. "You have to! I cannot go another year losing to St. Francis."

"My mom's going to be pretty livid I missed class today." Unless, of course, I got arrested first. Then it probably wouldn't matter so much.

"Maybe Mrs. Petrova hasn't input the attendance yet." Wootten backed up. "It's possible a call hasn't gone out to your mother yet. I need to see if I can stop her."

I blinked. "You'd really do that?"

"I think we can make an exception." Wootten made a stern face. "But just this one time." Then he took off toward the office. "Mrs. Petrova!"

As Wootten tore down the hall, I lost my sense of urgency. Either he'd stop the call or Ma would find out. I'd receive some serious Divine Intervention – which I highly doubted – or Keith would come for me. Either way, at this point, it didn't make much sense to catch the last half of English class.

I went to the washroom to change and then walked down the hall wondering what to do with myself. I rolled my eyes when I came to a destination. My first time skipping class and I chose to spend it in the library. I sighed and sat down behind a secluded computer.

I told Nate I'd do my best to help him. As long as I could, I might as well. I had some research I needed to do and it was just interesting enough to take my mind off… everything. I paused in the middle of logging into my account. This wasn't research I wanted traced back to me. It took me a couple tries to remember the password for the administrative account one of my teachers had given me to use to format a school newsletter. I opened a browser, and then sat, tapping a finger against my lips. How did someone go about researching penises?

26

Back when my class had learned about reproductive organs, Ma had demanded to scour through my health teacher's lesson plans and insisted I be pulled out of class. After what I'd heard were tough negotiations, Ma, my teacher and Principal Wootten agreed that I'd learn the parts and functions of a penis through a diagram but I'd be pulled out of class the day they looked at actual penises. Em, good friend that she is, offered to show me the pics, but that felt grossly unnecessary so I'd declined her kind offer. Now that I needed to research it and didn't know where to start, I totally regretted it. Who needed to be able to colour in and label a vas deferens when they couldn't even figure out if they'd seen a statue's penis?

My fingers hovered over my keyboard. I could straight up type in 'penis,' but I figured I'd get raunchy porn sites and I wanted serious genitalia. Penises befitting ancient fertility gods. I typed in 'ancient genitalia' and Google came back with 'Why do Greek statues have such small penises?,' articles on classical penis size, and more of the like.

Alright, I needed to be more specific. I typed in 'fertility god penises' and found a lot of hits on Priapus, the one Greek god who apparently did not have a small penis. From the drawing on Wikipedia it looked like a long, skinny sweet potato. My mouth wrinkled in distaste. Now every time I helped Ma peel and chop sweet potatoes, I'd think of Priapus.

"Hey, Asiya." Ronnie, a girl I hung out with briefly when Em was dating a hipster in the making, stood over my monitor. "I didn't know you had this period spare."

"I, um, actually, I'm just down here to do a little research for class." I kept my eyes on her as I reached discretely for the mouse.

"Lucky the teachers trust you so much." Ronnie smiled. "They'd never let me do something like that."

"I guess, yeah." I clicked to open a new window at the exact moment she bent, her brown eyes surveying the blank search box on my screen.

"So, what are you researching?" She asked.

"Uh, tuber vegetables."

Ronnie wrinkled her nose. "For which class?"

"English," I said. "I'm trying to find the perfect analogy for my... essay."

"That's really boring, to be honest." Ronnie, tucked a blonde highlight behind ear and eyed me shyly. "I heard something, about you and Michael?"

"Heard what?"

"Susan said she saw you two go to the hookup stairwell together?" She asked.

Great. Ronnie wasn't a gossip, so if she had heard, everyone else in school had too. The Mutaweenies might not talk to girls, but if everyone was talking about it, they'd eventually hear.

"Susan was mistaken. All we did was walk toward the exit at the same time." And talked together briefly before I ran like hell. No hooking up involved.

Ronnie watched me, fiddling with the ties of her peasant top, as she came to a decision over whether I was telling the truth. It seemed like she really wanted me to be, because she smiled and said. "Good." Relief obvious on her face, her gaze flicked to the monitor again. "Good luck with the tuber analogy. I'll leave you to it."

I didn't know what about Ronnie's interest in Michael felt weird to me. It's not like he was mine, and girls crushing on him was nothing new. I forced myself back to the screen and scrolled further through the results. Apparently anything other than ancient Greek penises weren't worth mentioning. Seriously, Google. Other ancient people had penises too. Could we perve on them for a bit, please?

I typed in 'African fertility god penises' and found Min, an ancient Egyptian god, who had the prerequisite charcoal looking skin, but he was dressed in a robe, and subsequently his penis was white. Well, that didn't help. I went back to scroll the rest of the results. Aaaaand we were back to Greek genitalia. Yeesh, Google. Fetish much?

Class was almost over, I couldn't do this research at home and I faced the fact that finding the exact ancient fertility god penis I may or may not be looking for was not going to happen. With a huff, I went to Google Images and typed in 'dick pics' before I could back out.

A pop-up flashed immediately: "Your search is in violation of school Internet usage policy. An alert has been sent to the office."

What! I stood, moving the mouse to click the browser closed at the same time. It wouldn't close.

Oh my God. I clicked and clicked and clicked and clicked and clicked, and it would not close.

I almost sprained a finger jabbing the power button on the computer tower to force a restart, and then ran for the farthest part of the school in case anyone came looking.

Despite roasting in fear, the rest of the school day went surprisingly okay in a Keith-didn't-charge-into-any-of-my-classes-to-lock-me-up kind of way. It would be just like him to prolong this in order to enjoy the process of tormenting me. Most likely he was waiting to do it at the *masjid* to make the most of his triumph. That thought helped me relax minimally. At least I had a couple days of freedom, kind of.

On the way home from school, I pulled out my phone and called Vicky.

"Asiya! Are you coming back? I swear to God this gazebo thing is killing me. I have to get permits from the city and the province and so many other things. I could really use the help. This has to get done!"

"Um, maybe this spring is too soon to expect it to be done?"

"It absolutely has to be," Vicky said. "I need it to have the perfect outdoor wedding."

I was pretty sure pushing permits through didn't work based on one woman's desire to have the perfect wedding, but I didn't say that. "You wouldn't consider moving your wedding back?"

I could almost hear Vicky shake her head. "I'm getting old."

I laughed. "No, you're not."

"I turned 35 this year."

Vicky was so fun I hadn't realized she was twice my age. But still. "Thirty-five isn't exactly old."

"It's getting there if you want to have a kid," Vicky said. "And I really do."

"I didn't know."

"Yeah," Vicky said softly. "I should have been a mother by now."

I wondered if Vicky had miscarried like Nasreen Aunty's daughter had, but it felt invasive to ask.

"Anyway." Vicky perked up, sounding like her usual self. "If you're not calling about coming back, what's going on?"

My mouth suddenly felt full of sand. I told myself to get it together. I had a possible penis to identify.

"So, that statue you saw the police take from Nate's office, the one with the missing penis, do you recall how tall it was?"

"By eyeball, I would say about a foot high. How come?"

"Oh, um." I could have just told Vicky I was helping Nate, but something about how quickly she'd accepted his guilt made me decide not to. "I'm researching fertility statues for a school project and since you recently saw one, I thought I'd ask you about them."

"Okay." Vicky laughed. "But I only got a quick look, and like I said, there wasn't much to see!"

"Do you think if there still had been something to see, it would have been erect?" I asked.

"Uh…hard to say."

"Well, how long do you think it would have been? Do you think it would look like a wooden snake broken in half?"

Vicky was silent for long enough for me to think she'd disappeared, then she sighed. "I may be old enough to be your mom, but just barely. I don't know why you didn't learn about this stuff in Sex Ed, but if you want to know about penises you're going to have to find someone else."

"No, Vicky, I –"

"Look Asiya, I've got lots of work to do. If nothing else, I'm sure one of the boys at school would be more than happy to help you with your *research*."

I let out a defeated sigh. I'd tried online and I tried on the phone. Vicky was right. I was going to have to ask a real live person.

27

When I got home from school, I entered carefully, not knowing what I'd find. What I hadn't expected was Nasreen Aunty sitting at the kitchen table chatting with Ma – Ma had socially banished herself after the masjid incident until now.

I faltered, not just because of Nasreen Aunty's presence, but because Ma looked like she might actually be happy to see me.

"School was good today?" she asked.

Uh-oh. She was up to something. I could tell by the way she pretended to care.

"Okay," I said carefully.

"Mr. Wootten has called," she said.

Oh God. I knew one way or another, things would come to this, but yeesh. Wootten had me believe he was looking out for me.

"He told me he's very excited to have you on the Quizbowl team," Ma said, looking a little too smug. "He says that the school may win with your help."

Oh. Ma invited Nasreen Aunty over to hear that so she could spread the gossip and start damage control. That couldn't be a bad thing. If Ma was planning on coming out of exile, that meant less time stuck at home with me.

"Ah." Nasreen Aunty nodded, totally seeing through Ma. "My Rina won two Quizbowls when she was in high school. But good for you for trying, Asiya. This will be a much better focus for you than being out and about with that boy, *nah?*"

And there was the storm cloud, back on Ma's face. Just as Nasreen Aunty expected, I was sure.

"I don't know what is happening to this city." Nasreen Aunty let out a long-suffering sigh. "It is as if it has lost its *barakah*, like when Mercer was here."

Sheriden was a prosperous, growing suburb. Despite Sue's murder, it was totally safe and Nasreen Aunty was just saying that to strike up drama.

I took a calming breath and I reminded myself I felt bad for her. After Rina married and left, she only had Tariq and Laddoo, her fat orange housecat, to keep her company at home. I even understood that she spent her days gossiping about people and coming over here to interfere in my life because she had no other purpose in hers. I told myself that since she was exactly the kind of woman I had nightmares about becoming I should be able to find a shred of compassion for her somewhere.

"Rina's so smart," I said, digging deep and ignoring that Nasreen Aunty's daughter was also so vain and superficial she made the perfect best friend for Afiya. "No wonder they won when she was on the team."

"Yes," Nasreen Aunty said, happy to accept the topic change since it always suited her to brag about Rina. "You have always done well in school. Maybe you will win too."

That crumb of confidence in me seemed to satisfy Ma. Which meant it was time to ask, "Ma, can Em come over? We want to start studying for Quizbowl together."

"Ah, Em is on Quizbowl too!" Ma said.

She wasn't but if I had to be there I'd make her join too. Em was a history rock star and her old history teacher was supervising the team. She'd have no trouble making the cut.

"Fair and pretty, and she is smart too!" Nasreen Aunty remembered Em from Afiya's wedding events.

"She is such a proper girl." Ma nodded as if I'd lucked out to find her. Which I totally had, but not in the way they thought. Em was the only person who was real with me. I could ask her about penises and she wouldn't even blink. And anyway, I wanted a last hang out with my best friend in case Keith came for me.

About an hour later, including ten full minutes of Ma and Nasreen Aunty fussing over Em, we finally made it to my room.

"Penis pictures are here!" Em exclaimed cheerfully the second my bedroom door closed.

"Shhh!" I pulled up a playlist on my phone. "Wait till the music is on."

"Here's the deal." Em put on her fierce face. "I've got unlimited data and we can look at all the dick pics you want, but first. I heard you were with Michael in the hookup stairwell, and then you didn't show up for lunch." Em waved her phone in my face. "If you want a taste of the man meat I've got on here, you'd better start talking."

My nose wrinkled. "Ok, fine."

Em practically squealed as she jumped up and down on my bed. "I'm so glad your mom let up. We haven't done this forever! I have stuff to tell you too, but first, give it up. Every. Last. Detail."

"Alright." I took a deep breath in and told Em everything. The truth from that first walk with Michael, including finding Sue's body, Michael going missing, lying to the police, searching Sue's apartment and finding the broken wood snake, lying to Keith and getting caught, Jamie covering for me and my parents being livid, calling Vicky and hearing about the penisless statue, avoiding Michael and how that failed, pretending to be Ma so I could go see Nate, and getting caught by just about everyone. "...so, you see, I think the wooden snake might be a castrated statue penis."

Em stared at me, still as... well, a penisless statue. She didn't move for so long I flicked my fingers in her face just to see if she'd blink.

"Let me get this straight," Em said starting to look fierce. "In the last two weeks, you lied to your parents repeatedly, lied to the police repeatedly, searched the apartment of a woman who was murdered, almost got arrested, then went on to commit identity fraud, and now you want to break into the murdered woman's apartment, *again,* so you can play pin the prick on the murder weapon, but you didn't really kiss Michael because *that* would be bad?"

"That's what you're going to focus on?"

"Ya-ya!"

"Okay." I admitted. "You have a point. But–"

"I can't believe this! I was so excited for you. I thought you wanted to have a look at the goods so you didn't freak out when Michael pulled out his pocket rocket!"

"What?" I physically backed away. "Why would you think that?"

"Oh, excuse me. You're right, my first thought should have been, 'Asiya wants to talk diddlesticks because she's mentally piecing together an ancient wooden erection!'"

Em was so upset she was flushed. Her body tight and her arms crossed.

"Em." I knew her well enough to understand the real issue. "I'm sorry I lied to you."

Em deflated immediately. "I'm sorry too. I shouldn't have assumed. I don't mean to push you." She sighed. "I just wish you'd open up with someone other than me."

"What are you talking about? I make friends with everyone you do."

"No, Ya-ya, you don't. You let them think you do, but you don't really let them get to know you," Em said, gently. "I thought things were different with Michael. But I guess I was wrong."

I ran my finger over the threads in the quilt my grandmother had embroidered. I wanted to leave Em with her wrong assumption, but I'd just made up with her for lying. "I like him." I admitted. "But I am not ready for that stuff. Forget sex, I can't even deal with the idea of someone's tongue in my mouth."

"So, you go slow, and if he pushes you for anything you don't want, you drop kick his ass out of your life. But just, give yourself a chance."

Fear, and maybe a tiny bit of excitement, at the idea that Michael and I were possible hummed through me. And then I remembered. "If one of the Mutaweenies at school ever saw me with Michael, it'd be game over."

"Are you sure they're that bad?"

I rolled my eyes. "They immunize themselves against Satanic sex infections by staying away from girls, and judging us from afar."

"They're in high school. They have hormones too. I bet they're going through the exact same thing as you."

"Not possible, but even if it were true, it wouldn't be the same because they're guys. They'd get a slap on the wrist and be told to lower their gaze. If I get caught, I'll be kept protected at home until after graduation, possibly longer." I shook my head. "The stakes aren't the same, so I can't trust them."

Em looked devastated, like she was more upset about the Mutaweenies than me.

I forced a smile. "Enough about that. What's exciting with you?"

"Nothing much."

"But you said–"

"Yeah, that was before I heard what's going on with you."

Em smiled, but I got the feeling her smile was about as genuine as mine had been a moment ago. "Tell me again, if you insist on returning to Sue's, why don't you just find the snake bit and bring it back with you. We can do the examination together."

"I can't, it's evidence."

"Then why not tell the police and let them look?" Em asked.

"Because if they find Sue's journal before I do, then Michael might never know about his mom," I said. "She's here, Em. In Sheriden. Nate told me Sue talked to her. If I can find the journal, maybe I can find out why she didn't want to see Michael."

Em looked skeptical. "You find the journal. And then what?"

"Then I'll call Jamie and let her handle everything."

"And Michael?"

"I'll decide after I see the journal," I said, even though I didn't know what I'd find that would change anything.

"Ya-ya." Em bit her lip. "You know you can't keep this from him."

I shook my head. "I can't tell him the mother he's been looking for his whole life doesn't want to see him."

"He's going to be devastated either way," Em said. "Even if you don't want to date him, be his friend for this. He's going to need you."

My heart thudded in my chest at the thought of talking to Michael. Ma must have been right about the whole Satan business, because the more I was with Michael, the less I wanted to be his friend.

28

I found Michael in Computers the next day. Once he spotted me through the glass in the classroom door, I moved further down the hall. A few moments later he was beside me.

"Hey," he said, sliding his hand into his pocket.

"Can we talk?"

The corner of Michael's mouth curved. "I've been hoping."

I couldn't get myself to smile back.

"What's wrong?" Michael asked immediately.

"I just…" I scanned the length of the currently empty hallway. "We should do this somewhere private."

Confusion crossed Michael's face, but he didn't ask. "There aren't a lot of places."

We headed to the hookup stairwell, Michael throwing curious glances my way, me throbbing inside at the hurt I was about to inflict on him.

"I went to see Nate yesterday." I blurted out the minute we got there.

"What?" Michael took a second, like he needed to replay what I said again to make sure I'd said it. "In jail? Why would you do that?"

"They're saying he had the murder weapon displayed in his office like a trophy. But he didn't. I checked his office after I checked out Sue's apartment for you last week and it wasn't there."

"It's been over a week, he could have killed her and put it there any time in between."

That was exactly what Keith had said. "I don't believe he did."

"I don't get why you would get involved after all the trouble you got in."

"I'm involved because Nate's innocent."

"You can't be sure," Michael said. "The police must have had something on him to arrest him."

That had me blink in confusion. "Now you trust the police?"

"No. I just think Nate could have really killed her. And okay… that one detective you told me about. She actually listened like she really wanted to help me." Michael took a deep breath. "I know you just want to help Nate. You care. I like that about you. It's just I've been so worried for you. Even before knowing you got in trouble with your parents, it's been killing me that I asked you to check Sue's apartment and I couldn't talk to you. I couldn't even call to see if you were okay."

Michael's eyes peered into mine, saying more than his words were. He lifted a hand to my face. "It scares me to think about something happening to you."

My hand reached up to grip his wrist. How did this get so off track? My fingers held on a few pulse beats before I could compel them to move his hand from me and let him go.

"There's something I have to tell you," I said, rushing to do it before I lost the nerve. "You were right. Your mom is in Sheriden.

Michael stilled. "How do you know?"

"Nate told me," I said. "Sue tried talking to her about you… but Michael," I took a deep breath and swallowed. "She doesn't want to see you."

"Wha… How…" Michael's laboured to take in a couple of erratic breaths. "You're sure?"

"Sue tried hard for you… but your mom was adamant."

Michael turned away then. "Thanks for telling me," he said without looking back. "You should go. Before you get in trouble."

I was already in trouble. I couldn't watch Michael's shoulders heave as he struggled with long breaths that didn't seem to go anywhere and just walk away. In that moment I felt so much rage toward the woman who gave birth to him. How could she? Michael was a good person. He deserved a mother who loved him. He deserved to have someone care.

"Michael."

He shook his head, refusing to face me. His clenched fist and forearm thudded against the cement wall and stayed there. His head hung low.

"Michael." I didn't wait for a response this time. I slid between him and the wall and wrapped my arms around him.

He hugged me back immediately, squeezing so hard I could barely breathe. Or maybe it was the pain I felt rolling off of him that was suffocating me. For a long time we stood there, him clutching me silently, his body shaking with the heavy breaths he took, me giving him what little solace I could.

I don't know after how long, but slowly, gradually, the tension drained from Michael's body and he loosened his hold. He gazed down at me, his eyes red and dry.

"I'm sorry," he said.

"Don't be." I smiled trying to lighten things. "Being in your arms isn't that difficult."

I heard what I'd said after I said it. My eyes dropped to Michael's chest. "I meant…"

"Asiya." Michael whispered. "If you don't want me to…" His words trailed off as his face lowered ever so slowly toward mine. He watched me, waiting to see, wanting to know I wanted this.

There was no denying I did.

A soft kiss swept the side of my bottom lip, spreading tingly shivers from where his lips met mine. His lips pulled away only to center on my mouth, this time firmer, like a sweet seal of him and me.

Sensations tingled from my mouth and face, down my entire body. Every second of his lips against mine flushed me through with a shivery warmth.

Warmth that faded to a glow as Michael inched back to take me in. Our lips had just been pressed together, but I couldn't keep my eyes on his. Probably because of that very reason, my gaze dropped between us.

Michael's fingers lit a blaze of sensation as they slid around my neck and threaded into my braid. It felt so good, my neck became jello-y and my head melted back into his palm, bringing my eyes back to his.

"I appreciate how close you and Em are." The corner of his mouth hooked into a ghost of smile as he ran a tantalizing thumb over my jaw. "But I can go as slow as you need. I don't need her to remind me to treat you like you're precious."

The haze of him and me dimmed and broke as a swift intake of breath drew my gaze over Michael's shoulder. Ali stood there looking as shocked as I felt.

I jerked out of Michael's arms, but the damage couldn't be undone. A Mutaweenie had seen.

29

It would serve that boy right to be put away." Patti glanced over at me. It was so weird to think of Nate's mom by her name. I'd been raised to respectfully defer to age. Even though she insisted, it was so hard not to mentally add 'aunty' every time I said Patti, like I did with my parents' friends.

Not only did Patti drive over to give me Sue's key, she offered to take me to her apartment and bring me back to school, which I'd gratefully accepted. It took some of the pressure off not to have to worry about getting myself back before the bell.

"The one thing I asked of him. I said to him, all I'm asking you for. All I want, after everything I've done for you is a couple of grandkids. And what does he do? He goes traipsing about nature."

"Nate really loves the woods." I agreed.

"I told him he could go traipsing about nature when he was old. He finally found a great girl. What he needed to do was get down on his knees and go traipsing through her bush."

My eyebrows shot up.

"Then he could have taken his time knocking her up. Not that Sue had any objections. But he should have done it for good measure. No girl in her right mind would keep a guy who's lacking in the generosity department. You hear me, Asiya?"

"Um. Yes, ma'am."

"Nate tells me you're the traditional type, but I'll tell you. Traditional or not, a girl's gotta get the guy who gives the giving good."

"I…"

"And I don't want to be hearing from Nate that you've got yourself a slacker. It's generous or nothing. You got that?"

"Trust me, you won't."

Patti sighed. "Nate will have to start all over now."

I was starting to think Patti was a little prone to memory loss… like forgetting that her son in jail, mourning the woman he loved.

Patti said, "But he'll have another chance after you get him out of jail."

Okay, she wasn't just forgetful. She was just plain crazy.

"Hopefully in a year or two, he'll be ready to try again."

"I don't want to give you the wrong idea," I said. "I know Nate didn't kill Sue, and I hope proof exists, but I can't promise you I'll find it."

Patti pulled into the parking lot, turned off the car and

stared straight ahead. "Until he gives me grandkids, he's all I've got. So, if it's alright with you, I'm just going to sit here and plan a future for my boy. As for you, there's no one else to ride in on a white horse, so you might as well get to it."

I took the stairs again, putting away my braid and pulling on my gloves while there. I slid Sue's key into the door and closed it quietly behind me. This time, I went straight to Sue's writing desk, pulled out the pens and emptied the jar. The wooden penis. I was almost sure of it. I took a few pictures with my phone and piled it and the pens back in the jar. I glanced up at Sue's collage of notes. Her collage of notes, minus one. The angry note from Sebastian was gone. I dropped down to look under the desk in case it had fallen. Nothing.

My mind raced through possibilities as I searched through the apartment twice. I wondered where it could have gone and who would have taken it as I opened each book on her shelf, looking for the journal I missed the last time I was here. It made me uneasy to know someone else had been in here. I sped through checking the books on her shelf. No luck.

I checked my watch. My heartbeat picked up and played loudly in my throat. Even with Patti's ride, I'd be late if I took much longer. Looking over everything I'd already scoured, I ended up in the kitchen. Just for the hell of it I pulled open Sue's cabinets, sorted through spice jars and peered behind pots. The last cabinet was a narrow one where Sue kept a black teapot with painted on floating cherry blossoms, matching cups and a few cookbooks. The books were high up, and I didn't want to risk dragging over a chair. I climbed up onto the counter and cracked each open. There it was. Sue's journal. Hidden under the cover of Homemade Mac and Cheese. Smart move. Why anyone would go through the effort of making mac and cheese from scratch when the processed version was so good?

The front door swung open. I hopped down, landing on the balls of my feet and staying crouched low on instinct. Footsteps paced into the apartment. My heart pounded so hard I couldn't think beyond its clamour.

"I know you're here."

I knew that voice. Scratchy, grumpy and ... the old dude from across the hall. Twice in a row was too unlikely. He must have been watching Sue's apartment. But why? And why was I trying to figure that out instead of how to get out of here?

I tucked Sue's journal into the back of my pants, and pulled my shirt down over it. If I could wait for him to get deeper into the apartment I might be able to dart past him and out the door.

"You're not going anywhere," he said, sounding like he stood right in the entryway.

Staying low, I moved carefully to peer into the living room. Yup, he was right in front of the *open* door. That was weird. If he wanted to do something wouldn't he prefer not to have witnesses? Not that I was going to give him the idea.

"I knew you were lying the last time you were here."

"Well, this time I caught you, you little delinquent. And the officer is going to be very happy I did."

He'd called the police? No wonder he wasn't closing the door. He had the law on his side. I had to get out of here *now*. But the only way out was through him. Could I do that? Could I hit an old guy? And how much force would it take to knock him over and get away, but not actually hurt him?

"Swiss Aunt in the building." He snorted. "Like I'd believe that."

Okay, it could hurt a little bit... but could I really do this? I looked down to my hands. They were shaking. I tried willing them to stillness. Okay, maybe not. But all I really needed was strong legs. I'd charge him, yelling like a Viking, and scare him still before I bowled him over and made it out free. That's what I was going to do. I was. On one, two, three.

"Ahhhhh!" I shot out from the kitchen. The old dude jumped in shock and slumped down to the ground.

Patti stood smiling behind him, a frying pan in her hand. She tossed it across the hall, I assumed back into his place. "Of course, I ride pretty damn well myself," Patti said. "And not just the white ones either, if you know what I mean."

I was pretty sure I did, but I was so happy to see her I laughed anyway as I grabbed her hand and dragged her behind me. "Come on, Patti Aunty. We've got to get out of here now. The police are on their way."

I was yanked to a stop when Patti stilled. She stared at an empty shelf. "The fertility statues I gave Sue are gone?"

"Sue kept the statues on that shelf?" I asked.

Patti shook herself out of it and answered as she rushed to the car with me. "Everyone knows fertility statues can't do their magic if they're not in the bedroom with you. But Sue didn't want Nate to feel pressured, and she didn't want me to feel bad, so she compromised by keeping them in the living room."

My mind raced with possibilities as we jumped into the

car.

Patti shook her head and pulled out of the parking lot. "That woman was too good to die like that."

Killed in her own living room with a statue that represented hope for new life. Sue definitely deserved better.

By the time Patti dropped me back to school I was twenty minutes late for English, but at that point I didn't care. I waited at the same side door, and weirdly the same guy, Isaac, happened to be walking by and opened it for me. I rushed down the hall, thanking God for letting this adventure go successfully if not smoothly. *Honestly God, after the whole Keith* and *Wootten catching me thing, I was starting to think You hated me.*

I rounded the corner filled with a sense of accomplishment. I had the journal, God didn't hate me, and I was sure I could explain away twenty minutes to Mr. Mathis. Or I would have if I'd gotten to him.

I halted like I'd hit a glass wall. Because in front of my English class stood Principal Wootten. And beside him was Ma.

30

With absolute precision, as if her mother's intuition was finely tuned to the smell of my fear, Ma's neck rotated and her gaze zeroed in on me. I could feel the heat of her seething anger from 15 metres away.

"Asiya." Wootten strode toward me. Ma took her time following.

My face must have shown my horror, because Wootten put on a particularly fake, cheery smile. "Asiya, good news! Your mother isn't as unreasonable as you think."

A boulder of lead started a slow descent down my stomach. I couldn't look at Ma, but I could feel her gaze searing me.

"She came to discuss exactly what will be required of you to participate in the Quizbowl." The thought put a real smile on Wootten's face. "I think this will all work out really well. Assuming of course, your absence yesterday and your tardiness today are aberrations."

God, could things get any worse?

And then the door to my English class opened and closed, and Michael came rushing toward me.

I looked up to the ceiling. *I'm sorry for doubting You, God. I bow down to your Infinite Power. Of course, You can make things worse.*

Michael sized up the situation. He stopped on the spot.

Leave! I screamed inside my head. *Run before–*

Wootten turned, drawing Ma's gaze with him. "Michael," he said.

Really God, I believe. No more need to demonstrate.

Ma stiffened at his name. She assessed him with shrewd eyes.

Wootten frowned. "Where are you going?"

Michael's eyes met mine for the slightest moment – which of course Ma caught – before he said, "The washroom."

I dared take the slightest breath. That was plausible.

"Closest one is that way." Wootten nodded toward the other direction.

Aggghhhh!

"Yes sir," Michael said, rounding back toward a washroom he obviously didn't need to use.

Ma's eyes narrowed as she watched Michael skulk away.

I could still explain this. Just because we were both out of class at the same time didn't have to mean–

"I don't know what's happening." Wootten shook his head. "It's like all of my best students are always trying to get out of class these days."

You hate me don't You, God?

Wootten rounded back to me. "No more missing class for you, young lady. Now that you're on our Quizbowl team, you can't afford to miss any more learning."

I tipped my head in acknowledgement. Ma would definitely encourage me to get back to class.

The minute Wootten turned away, she reared on me. "You think you are so smart? That your mother and father are stupid? That we will continue to believe your lies while you skip school to be with that *shadha goonda*?" Ma shook her head in disgust. Her face twisted with revulsion, she practically spit the words, "What a dirty girl. Who will ever call you proper after this?"

With that, Ma turned and left for home, and I went to English, trying not to think about what I'd be facing when I got there.

31

I'm sorry." Michael hunched down next to my desk the second Mr. Mathis left us to discuss whatever lesson I'd missed so far in English. "I didn't mean to—"

"You couldn't have known," I said. And I had no way to explain it to him. How different my world was from his. How stupid I was to think this could ever work.

Michael took my hand in both of his under the desk. His warm hands cradled my cold one. "Tell me what I can do."

"Nothing," I said, knowing with certainty that it was true.

Em lived in a fairytale world thinking that Michael and I could happen. Even if Ma hadn't seen it for herself, Ali had and word would have eventually gotten to her.

"I can't change things," I said, staring at the chalkboard ahead. "I can't live a life I don't have."

"I know right now everything keeps coming down on you,

but we'll figure it out." Michael squeezed my hand. "There's something right about this. You know it too."

What I knew was we were fighting the inevitable, and I was getting slaughtered along the way. "We need to stop."

"Don't say that." Michael's hand tightened on mine, but I didn't think he realized.

I blinked back tears. It was hard enough telling an amazing guy who had no one that you didn't want him either. "Don't make me have to say it again."

I took a steadying breath and turned to look him in the eyes before I slid my hand from between his. I already missed his warmth. "If you care at all, you'll stay away."

I spent the rest of English rapidly blinking. At one point, I pulled out Sue's journal to lose myself in someone else's problems, but I could feel Michael's gaze on me so intensely, I couldn't keep reading. Ditto for Mrs. Lee's class. She had particularly keen eyes and a tendency to keep things that shouldn't have been brought to class.

After school, I made it out of the crowded halls in a haze. I heard Ali calling after me. I had two guesses what he wanted to talk about, and I wasn't interested in either. I pretended not to hear him.

I had much to avoid thinking about on the walk home, so I finally took out Sue's journal and flipped through, stopping the second I spotted Michael's name.

Sometimes I hate this job so much, I can't stand it. I can't take it that I know the right thing to do and my hands are tied to do it. How many more times is Michael going to come back? It tears me apart every time I have to turn that boy away. Not just because of him, but because of who he reminds me of....

An engine roared behind me. Teens lucky enough to have fancy supped up rides and the freedom to use them weren't uncommon in Sheriden. It was the sound of a car's suspension swinging so close that alerted me to something off. I jerked around, just in time to catch sight of a car jump the curb. And run straight at me.

32

I could hear Ma yelling, but something was wrong with her yells. Like someone had turned the volume down on them. And the cement determination usually in her voice had been wiped away, or at least watered down.

"I will walk her to school and back myself," Ma said, semi-fiercely.

The horror of that idea made my eyes pop open.

"Unh?" I blinked back against the bright lights of the... hospital room?

"Asiya." Abbu's hand stroked carefully over my hair. "How are you feeling?"

It hit me just as he asked. I felt horrible. Sore in some places, scraped in others, and my head pounded, but I went with, "my foot hurts."

"It's swollen and the doctor said you have a hairline

fracture," Abbu said. "A car hit you."

My eyes widened as I remembered. "My book." I searched the room frantically for Sue's journal. I tried to sit up and failed to find the energy. "Where is my stuff?"

"Asiya," Ma said slowly. "You do not need to study at the hospital."

Study?

Ma nodded. "You can wait until you get home."

"You're not studying this weekend," Abbu said. "And we sent your stuff with Adil to Nasreen's house. He was very worried about you, so we thought it would be a good idea to keep him busy."

I wanted to call Adil right away to see if the journal was there, but I couldn't because my parents refused to leave my side. The doctor came by and checked on the swelling in my foot, told me I'd have to use crutches to keep the pressure off for a while, and informed me I had a mild concussion.

Ma listened, her eyes filled with tears and possibly a resolve to not only keep me in the house from now on, but contained within a plastic bubble as well. Just as the doctor was finishing up, Jamie knocked at the door.

"I'm sorry to push," Jamie said to Ma and Abbu, "but I really need to talk to Asiya. The longer we wait, the less chance we'll find who did this to her."

Abbu nodded and went to take the chair next to me.

"Asiya's been through a lot," Jamie said. "She might be more likely to remember something if she's not so stressed." She glanced discreetly at Ma, who still hovered at my bed side, doubly overwrought by the doctor's visit. "I'm sure you both can use a cup of tea yourselves."

Abbu looked like he was going to object, but I insisted that I'd be okay. Once they'd left, Jamie indicated my leg with her chin, "What's the damage?"

"A hairline fracture," I said, a little anxious about talking to Jamie. Keith must have told her by now that I'd been at the jail. Did she know I'd impersonated Ma?

She assessed my visible bruises and scratches. "You're lucky from what I hear."

"I don't feel lucky."

"Sometimes luck is a matter of perspective," Jamie gave me the slightest smile. "You can at least be happy that Keith didn't come in for his shift today. I'm sure you can do without the anger and accusations."

"I could do without him on any given day." A yawn forced itself out of my mouth.

"I know you're tired," Jamie said. "I'll ask you a few questions and let you rest, okay?"

I went to nod and found my head didn't like that. "Okay."

Jamie pulled a writing pad out of her pocket. "Can you tell me what happened after school today?"

"I was walking home," I said. "I heard this car coming and I turned just in time to see it. I remember trying to get out of the way, but," I looked down at myself in the hospital bed, "I must not have made it."

Now that Jamie was on the job, she was too focused to appreciate my joke. "Did you see what kind of car it was? Or notice anything about the driver?"

"I wish," I said. "But I can't remember anything."

"Even the tiniest detail can help."

"I think the car might have been blue or grey or something like that, but I'm not sure. It happened too quick."

"Okay," Jamie said. "Now this might have been an accident. It happens: drunk drivers, or just people who get distracted at the wheel, lose control, hit someone, and then run when they see what they've done. But I have to ask, can you think of anyone who might have wanted to hit you, deliberately I mean?"

I could tell her. I could tell her all of it. Let her deal with it and not have to worry about any of it.

"Asiya, if there's anything you can tell me that will help me find out who did this to you, you need to do it now," Jamie said. "The sooner we know what we're looking for, the more likely we can find the car."

I wanted to tell her. So badly. But I still didn't know what the journal said about Michael. And what about Nate? At this point, I didn't even know if I still had it. It didn't make sense to worry my parents more than I already had by admitting everything if I didn't have to. Which meant I needed to hold out on my own for just a little bit longer.

"I have no idea," I said.

"Okay," Jamie said, softly. She put her pad away. "Just know that if you come up with anything, you should call me right away."

I planned to do that as soon as possible. "I appreciate that."

"Khushie, you cannot homeschool her for university." Abbu's voice carried into my room a moment before he and Ma entered. "There are regulations to be followed."

Of course, now Jamie showed signs of a smile. "I should get back to work."

Abbu walked out with Jamie, no doubt looking for an update on what I'd said. Leaving me with Ma, who put her tea down on the table and came to stand by me. From the look on her face, the getting-hit-by-a-car reprieve was over. It was time for my reckoning.

33

Ma surveyed me, her face tight. "I told you you should not walk alone, did I not?"

"Ma," I said. But my gentle assurances caught in my throat. For once, I couldn't tell her everything would be okay.

"Now you see what has happened?" Tears spilt over Ma's bottom lids and down her face.

"Jamie said it could have been an accident." I grasped for anything to console her.

"Jamie does not understand how my heart clenches when I hear the daughter I have spent my life raising after thirty-two hours of labour to deliver her has been hit by a car." Ma's words were garbled from sobbing and talking at the same time.

As much as I wanted Ma to get used to the idea of letting me go, I didn't try to counter. This was the closest she'd come to saying something caring about me in forever.

"Until you are married, it is my responsibility to watch over you."

And then she had to go and say that.

"From now on I will watch over you every minute."

And that.

"The doctor has signed your release papers." Abbu entered with papers in hand.

Thank you, God.

"I should call Adil," I said. The sooner I found out about the journal the better.

"You can talk to him when he gets home," Abbu said. "He's at the masjid by now."

Adil might have the journal. Most likely, he was safe at the masjid, but there was no way I was risking it.

"I want to go," I said, "to the masjid."

Abbu looked at me as if… I'd hit my head.

"I should thank God. You know," I shrugged a shoulder, "that I'm okay." *Also, thank you God. You might not like me much, but I can still admit that this could have turned out much, much, worse.*

"The world is your masjid." Abbu quoted a saying of the Prophet. "You can thank Allah from your bed."

Since when had Abbu become the difficult parent? His moderate interpretations of faith were not helping me right now. I turned to Ma. "Please Ma? I have," I cleared my throat, wondering if she had the time to tell Abbu about me skipping… and Michael, again, "so much to repent for."

Ma's face hardened at the reminder. "That is true."

"I did not know you had become a Catholic," Abbu said

casually.

I tried to follow but, "I don't get it."

"You need neither a church or a priest to repent," Abbu sounding particularly irritated. "If you want forgiveness, mean it when you tell us you are sorry, and then do better."

Yup, Ma had definitely told him.

"I know I don't need to go," I said, grasping for something, anything, "but I just got hit by a car. I could have died alone on the street. Would it be so bad to go be with my community for a bit before going home?"

Ma dropped a hip on the bed and wrapped a protective arm around me. "She finally asks to go to the masjid. She wants to pray! In this, you must stand in her way?"

Abbu tried to engage me, asking with his eyes what was really up.

I looked away. He'd been an absent parent the entire week. There was no need for him to start getting all involved now.

"Okay." I heard Abbu say. "She wants to go to the masjid, we'll go."

Much later, thanks to the crutches that slowed me down, we made it to the masjid. I kept wanting to ditch the sticks and just hop along with my ankle boot, but the doctor had said the crutches and keeping my foot elevated were necessary until the swelling went down.

It wasn't until we got to the masjid that I realized I wouldn't be able to sit on the floor with Firdous and Leyan. Nope. I sat at the back with my leg across a chair to one side, and Nasreen Aunty on the other.

As if that wasn't bad enough, Alweenie decided today's

lecture should be about 'free mixing among the youths' and all the trouble it leads to. It was obvious to anyone who'd been here last week and anyone who'd heard, which was everyone present, that the whole thing was a thinly veiled admonition for me.

I let my eyes wander, doing my best to ignore Alweenie. Until he said, "Our young brothers and sisters must remember that Allah, the Most-High, tells us in the Holy Qur'an that 'you are indeed in Our eyes.'

"What is more, Allah has given the female an extra responsibility, a seal to ensure that she stays pure," Alweenie said. "And it is upon her to stay away from those who would seek to break her seal of purity. She must avoid situations where it will be threatened, such as being alone in the woods with a boy."

Did he just talk about *my hymen* in front of the whole congregation? How in the world did almost getting arrested for walking through the woods with a guy and lying about it equate with my hymen being threatened? In what universe did a walk through the woods mean sex? I mean other than Bollywood movies? I'd sat through some pretty messed up Alweenie nonsense, but this messed up Alweenie nonsense was personal.

Nasreen Aunty seemed to think the link was stellar because she nudged my bruised shoulder to make sure I was listening. As if it were possible for me to miss it. I couldn't believe I'd begged to come here on the one night I had a free pass away.

Alweenie's lecture reached a crescendo with a rallying war cry. "It must be protected at all costs!"

I breathed deep to ease the pressure building at the back of my head and focused my attention on drilling awareness into the back of Adil's head. When he finally turned and caught my eye. I subtly tilted my head to the exit. He nodded that he got my cue, *hallelujah!...* or uh, *Alhamdulilah!* Adil finally got a clue!

"I have to go do *wudhu*." I whispered to Nasreen Aunty as I pushed myself up, hopped around for my crutches and wondered why I'd said *wudhu* instead of the washroom. People only needed to re-cleanse after discharging some form of bodily function. Now, Nasreen Aunty probably thought I passed a silent backdraft while sitting with my butt directed at her. Oh well.

I met Adil out in the main hall.

"You gonna be okay *Apa*?" Adil asked, handing me my school bag. His round, worried eyes reminded me of when as a toddler, he'd first realized that for every cookie we ate, there was one less in the package.

"Yeah." I tucked a crutch under my armpit to reach over and ruffle his hair. "I'm going to be fantastic."

I convinced Adil he could and should head back before the parents came looking for us. I yanked my bag open and rummaged through it. Notebooks, textbooks, and other school stuff, but no journal. Either the journal was on the ground where I'd been hit, or − I faced the likely option − someone had hit me, possibly tried to kill me − to get the journal.

Exhausted and head hurting, I dropped onto a window alcove and let my crutches clatter to the floor. This was too much. I was just supposed to get the journal, see if it mentioned

Michael, and if there was anything Sue wrote that could help Nate. But now… Who even knew I had the journal? Just Patti, and possibly the old dude… I reached to the back of my neck, rubbing at the stiffness there. The old dude had said something weird, right after calling me a delinquent. Something about an officer being happy. Why would he have called an officer, instead of the police in general?

"I almost forgot." Adil came rushing back. He reached into the massive pocket of his baggy skate shorts and pulled out Sue's journal.

I wilted at the sight of it.

"I told the people at the hospital it wasn't yours, but they said the person who called the ambulance found it on you."

"It's mine." I practically snatched it from Adil's hand. "I, um, started journaling."

"Okay, Apa," Adil said. "But for Ma and Abbu I'd go with, 'I'm reading it for school.' It's easier to get off their radar when you give them what they want to hear."

I watched my baby brother shuffle back toward the prayer area. When had he started growing up?

I turned back to the journal in my hands and flipped open to the page I'd been reading earlier.

…Not just because of him but because of who he reminds me of.

The sound of slow, shuffling footsteps pulled me out away from Sue's words. Ali came to a stop in front of me. "Uh, are you okay?"

"I'm fine."

"I, um, wanted to talk to you about Michael."

"No." Not now. Not ever. I refused to put up with this policing bullshit, especially from a guy who talked to girls himself at school.

"You should know–"

"Don't try to tell me what I should know," I said.

"But I have to tell you about yesterday, at the stairwell–"

"Ali, let me make it clear. Do not talk to me. Just go away."

"But yesterday Michael insisted on driving me home. He–"

"– I don't want to hear–"

"– spent the whole time asking about–"

I hopped up on one foot and got in Ali's face. "I don't want to talk to you about Michael! I have enough people telling me what I've done and what I should do and I've had it. You are just a guy I see around the masjid and school. We don't talk. We're not friends. I barely even know you. So, you have no right to come up to me and tell me what I should or shouldn't do about anything!"

"Ali?" A woman's voice called from down the hall.

Ali's mother approached and Ali jumped back immediately. His mother's frown made it clear she'd noticed the lack of space between us a moment ago.

"Ali. *Baba*?" His mother flicked a stern glance in my direction. "What are you doing here?"

"We were just talking, mom." Ali almost whined. "Just about something at school."

"With *this* girl?" she asked, her face snarled. Her voice was filled with all kinds of surprise and disapproval. "Go back inside, *Baba*. You're missing Imam Alwanee's lecture."

Ali looked at me like he wanted to say something more, but hung his head and went back inside.

As soon as Ali was out of hearing distance, his mom turned on me. "And you! You are the one who needs to hear this lecture the most!"

"Ali was the one who came to talk to me."

"Don't you accuse Ali of starting this," she said. "I know exactly what you are doing. You go running through the woods with that criminal boy, and Allah knows who else. And now that you are ruined, you are trying to get a good Muslim boy hooked so he feels forced to marry you."

"What!?" My head hurt so much and she was so stupidly annoying. If she wasn't an Aunty, I would have swatted her.

"Don't act innocent." She gave me a cocky, I'm smarter than you look. "I am not new to this game."

Uh, eww. I hoped she wasn't implying... I didn't want to think about what she was implying.

"You can give up now, because you will not get anywhere near my *Baba*."

"Asiya." Abbu's voice entered the conversation. "Are you feeling okay?"

My head actually felt like it could explode, but that probably had to do with the deluded woman with the brain of a fruit fly in front of me.

Ali's mom narrowed her eyes at me – like it was my fault she got caught being a raging bitch – before smiling at Abbu. "*Bhai*," She said in a voice ten times softer and sweeter than she'd used with me. "I was just talking to Asiya about Imam Alwanee's speech."

Wow, I was *this* girl (said with a snarl), yet Abbu was 'brother'? I rolled my eyes. She must think Abbu was an idiot to fall for that.

"If you like it so much," Abbu told her, "you'd do better to go inside and listen."

Ali's mom scowled, but didn't say anything back to Abbu. She threw another ragey look in my direction and took off.

"It's time to go home." Abbu watched me rub the back of my head. "Unless you have not yet had your fill of the community?"

34

"Can we never come back here?" I asked Abbu as we moved to the car at a snail's pace thanks to me. He'd already told Adil that he and Ma should get a ride home with Nasreen Aunty before coming to find me. Abbu handed me a bottle of water and reminded me to take my pills before starting the car.

"You know that verse Imam Alwanee cited?" Abbu said. "The one 'you are indeed in Our eyes.' That's only part of it. The entire verse is 'Be patient for the decision of your Lord, for you are indeed in Our eyes. And exalt your Lord with praise when you arise.'"

I read out the dosage and swallowed down the pills. "If he's just cherry-picking verses to say whatever he wants, why do we bother coming here?"

"This is the only masjid in Sheriden and he is the Imam," Abbu said. "And despite his shortcomings, I thought you would like the verse."

I did like the hope in it, but I refused to admit it because Alweenie had brought it up. I scowled. "I hate Imam Alweenie."

I heard a small but distinct snicker and realized what I'd said. "Well, he is a weenie."

"Yes," Abbu said. "But a halal one."

"Are you seriously going to joke about this? He's always been stupid, but now he's outright attacking me." I crossed my arms. "I don't want to come back anymore."

"We come as a family so you will too."

"You don't even agree with half of what he says!"

"I agree that my daughter should not be mixing with boys."

I shut my eyes in frustration. "I don't know how much you heard, but I am *not* into Ali."

"I know." I could feel Abbu's eyes on me. "It's Michael you skip school and lie to your parents for."

Actually, no, but bringing up Nate didn't seem like a good idea. My head hurt too much to try to explain anything.

"We send you to school to get educated and this is what you do?" Abbu asked, his voice charged with quiet anger. "You skip class to spend time with this boy?"

"I wasn't with him."

"Try again." Abbu snapped.

"I'm telling you, I wasn't!"

"You've been telling us a lot of things," Abbu said.

"Well, this is the truth."

"You don't seem to know how to tell the truth anymore," he said. "Be honest, is Michael your boyfriend?"

Honestly? I wished. I wished so bad he could be, but I gave

him up because of them. And I still had to go through this? I didn't even know what Abbu expected me to say. When I said, Michael wasn't with me, he didn't believe me. Nothing I said mattered to him anymore.

"You promised me once you were done with Michael. That you'd put your family first. You already got caught skipping school. Now you want us to believe you weren't with him?"

"Fine," I said. Since he wasn't going to believe me anyway, I gave Abbu what he wanted to hear. "I was with Michael. He's my boyfriend." I choked on the words as I fought to push out the lie. "Is that what you wanted to hear?"

Abbu must have heard something off in my voice, because he glanced over at me. His fingers tensed on the wheel for a second, then he lifted a hand and placed a palm in front of me. "Let me see your phone."

I gave Abbu a questioning look, but handed it to him. Abbu held the phone against the wheel in front of him and scrolled through my recent calls and texts.

"You're going to get a ticket for driving and using a phone." I told him.

Abbu didn't take his eyes of the screen. "Now you're interested in following rules?"

I shut my mouth and stared out the window.

Abbu tossed the phone onto my lap. "No calls, no texts?"

"So?"

"You're so excited to see this boy, you have been skipping school to spend time with him and you don't talk to him outside of school?"

"You're the one who said I have a boyfriend," I said. "You

tell me how it's supposed to work."

Abbu sighed. "I learned with my first daughter what lies come out when she has a boyfriend."

Afiya had a boyfriend? I perked up at the news that she wasn't perfect, then deflated. If Abbu knew, then Ma knew. Only Afiya could get caught having a boyfriend and still have Ma's unwavering love.

"Asiya." Abbu looked aged, tired, and sad, like he was recognizing what things had come to. Like he was also remembering a time when I would tell him stuff I was too scared to tell Ma. "If Michael has gotten you into more trouble, you must tell me."

Enough with Michael! I had bigger things going on than him right now. I could tell Abbu, but self-preservation insisted I call Jamie in private, hoping that she'd do what she had to do without telling my parents.

"Talk to me old friend." Abbu prodded gently.

Even if I did tell Abbu, assuming he believed me, he'd still tell Ma. I would be beyond stupid to volunteer for her wrath. Just like with Imam Alweenie's attack on me, Abbu wouldn't do a thing to stop it.

"Michael doesn't like talking on the phone." I shrugged. "We just hang out at school. That's enough."

Pulling into the driveway, Abbu turned to face me. "You're not telling me the truth."

I stared at the garage door. "You already said I don't know how."

"Asiya, tell me what is happening with you!"

"Why?" I turned to face him as I blindly stabbed at the

button to release my belt. "Why do you suddenly care?"

"It's my job to take care of you. Even though you are making it hard to do so." Abbu's face softened. "What happened to you? Where did my *mishty* girl go?"

His gentleness took me back to all the times he'd been there for me. Knowing that time was over made my eyes prick with tears, and my body fill with resentment. I absolutely hated that he could make me cry with just two words.

"I am *not* your *mishty* girl." I shoved open the car door and hobbled out. "We are not friends, and lately you suck at your job."

35

Fighting with Abbu had depleted what was left of my energy and the drugs kicking in sapped me beyond bodily functioning. There was no way I was making it up the stairs myself and I was not asking Abbu for help. I dropped my bag on the living room floor, flopped down on the blanket covered couch and pretended to sleep.

I heard Abbu come in a little while later. It was so like him to get a hold of his anger before trying again. I felt him stand over me for a few moments before sitting in the armchair next to me. I knew he was waiting for me to admit I wasn't asleep. Well, he could keep waiting, because I wasn't done being angry. I knew exactly what I was going to do. The second he went upstairs, I was going… I was going to take out Sue's journal and read. I wished he'd go soon, because I was so tired. I needed… to sleep, but I needed to read. First. I needed to read, because something... something important about Michael. Michael was like someone... Who could he be like? I didn't know. Sue knew. I needed to read... so I could know... and... and.... and....................

I woke, still on the couch, with the quilt from my bed draped over me. I reached down into my bag, fished around and pulled out my dying phone. It was past one in the morning. I couldn't believe I'd fallen asleep. I must have slept through Ma and Adil coming home. At least my head felt better, if a little groggy.

I reached down to my bag again – Ma must have left it for me in case I wanted to study first thing after waking up – and pulled out Sue's journal.

I opened to the page I'd been reading,

... every time I have to turn that boy away. Not just because of him, but because of who he reminds me of.

Sebastian would have done anything to be a Keith, like his big brother. He begged me to get him away from his criminal father, but I couldn't help him get away. So, he decided he might as well truly become his father's son. I don't think either he or Keith will ever forgive me for that.

A Keith. What did Sue mean, by that? And why did I get the funny feeling she wasn't referring to just any Keith, but Constable Keith? I flipped back through the journal, scanning for another mention of either of them. I didn't find anything until almost a year back.

I saw Sean today. I drove by as he approached a car he'd

pulled over. I was so shocked I forgot to steer for a second and I thought I'd drive into him. I guess I shouldn't be surprised he'd become a police officer. After fighting so hard to get Sebastian away from their miscreant of a father and losing, it made sense that he wanted to feel like he had the power to go after criminals.

A little too eager, if you asked me. But then, despite his promise to come after me, he hadn't. Not even at the masjid today, and I knew how much he liked that.

I wished I could have stopped to tell him how proud I was of him for doing something positive with his life. And how sorry I was for how things ended for Sebastian.

Keith's brother was dead? My heart started thumping in my chest and I couldn't slow it or the flow of thoughts flooding my head. Keith had a really strong reason to hate Sue. Not only that, he was in the perfect position to get away with a murder… and frame Nate for it. Especially if he was the one who'd questioned Nate – he'd know exactly how to fill in the story to frame him. Keith had sworn he'd come for me once he found out what I was up to at the jail. It shouldn't have taken more than a few minutes to see Ma's name on the log. He'd hated me from the start. He should have relished coming after me, but he hadn't… at least not to arrest me. Hadn't Jamie said he'd missed his shift this afternoon? He'd taken time off exactly when I'd been hit by a car? That couldn't be a coincidence.

A sound outside pulled my attention. I rolled over, landing with an oomph behind the coffee table out of pure paranoia. A shot of pain tweaked through my foot, reminding me the swelling might have improved some, but my foot still wasn't fond of pressure. I waited a few seconds, listening closely and hearing nothing before slowly peeking over the table. I caught the back of a figure, a tall, lanky one, as it passed by my living room window.

36

This couldn't be for real. I swallowed. *God, could You please flip the channel on my life from horror to Disney for a bit? Anything over being in an episode of the dude from the Archie comics going on a murderous rampage.*

I shifted, searching the carpet for the phone I'd dropped in my mind-numbing fear. I pressed in 911, then backtracked. I was...known at the police station. There was no way they'd take my word over Keith's.

I shuffled through my contacts and tapped on Jamie's number, grateful she'd insisted I put it into my phone. I prayed she was awake.

"Shahid? What is it? Did something happen with Asiya?"

"Jamie." I breathed in relief. "It's me, Asiya. I'm not okay. Keith is... he's here outside my house. I... he... Jamie, he's the one who killed Sue."

Silence and then, "How do you know that?"

"I knew there was something off about Nate's arrest, so I went back to Sue's." I could feel Jamie's censure over the phone, but it was too late to worry about that. "I found her journal and there's all this stuff about how Sue failed to help Keith's brother and then, I think he died or something… I don't know. I didn't read all of it, but I know Keith hates her. He hates Sue and he totally could have planted the statue on Nate, and now he's after me. Jamie, you have to come stop him!"

"I'm coming." Lovely sounds of her hustling to get here came through the line. "But Asiya I can't just arrest him on your word. I'm sorry, but you're not exactly a trustworthy source. I'm going to need to take you and the journal to the police station."

"Okay." I swallowed. I wasn't looking forward to explaining this to my parents. "I'll wake up my parents."

"Have you told them any of this yet?" Jamie asked.

"No," I said.

"Anything at all?"

"Nothing."

"Then don't wake them. They're safer at home," Jamie said. "If what you're saying is true, then right now, Keith is only trying to silence you. If he thinks your family knows anything that will implicate him, he'll go after them too."

Oh God, I'd brought this on them. I put Ma and Abbu and Adil in danger.

"I want you to wait by your front door with the lights off," Jamie said. "I'll have the station call Keith in. Do not leave your house until I pull up, got it?"

"Okay," I said, even though none of this felt okay. Being in the same building as Keith, even a police station, was not high on my list of preferences right now.

Jamie must have heard the fear in my voice. "Asiya, don't worry. I won't let Keith anywhere near you."

Scared I'd pee myself in Jamie's car, I stayed low doing a one-legged crab walk over to the downstairs washroom. Jamie was pulling up in my front drive just as I got out.

Fear pounded through me. Something screamed inside me not to leave without telling Ma and Abbu, but I couldn't be selfish about this. Telling them would pull them into the danger that I'd brought on.

I grabbed my crutches and the journal and after a deep breath opened the front door. I wished Jamie would get out of the car and make sure Keith didn't shoot me in the back or something while I locked the front door. Or at least turn on her headlights so I could see better to slide in my key and lock the door. Jamie took off the second I slid my crutches in the back seat and hurtled into the passenger side.

"Thank you for coming, I…"

"Where's the journal?"

I pulled it out from under my shirt where I'd tucked it while I locked the door.

Jamie grabbed it and dropped it into the pocket of the driver side door.

"So how is this going to work? I'll give my statement and you'll go through the journal, and then go get Keith?" Ma and Abbu would be up for the dawn prayer in a few hours. I touched the phone in my pocket. I'd have to call them before then, or they'd have total meltdowns to wake up and find me gone. "How long do you think it'll be until I can call my parents?"

Jamie took a hard turn without slowing down. My crutch fell from the back seat and thwacked something on the car floor.

"Is Keith behind us?" I looked back, first out the back window to see nothing, then down to where my crutch had fallen. The big-boobed upper half of a charcoal fertility statue peaked out from under the back of Jamie's seat. The illumination of a passing streetlight showed a dark sticky substance glistening over the statue's head.

"Keith won't be coming." Jamie's voice was cold and impersonal.

So was the gun she had pointed at me.

37

I huddled back against the passenger door. "You killed Sue."

"Don't look at me like that." Jamie commanded.

I had no idea what was on my face, but I immediately tried to rearrange it so I didn't piss off the woman with the gun.

"Sue was going to crack. I could see it."

"Oh, my God, *you're* Michael's mom?"

Jamie glared at me, her eyes gleamed an icy green. "Judge all you want, but if she told Michael, it would have gotten out. And then his father would know. I did it to protect Michael!"

Protect Michael. From his father? And just like that, Sue's words came back. 'It tears me apart every time I have to turn that boy away... Not just because of him but because of who he reminds me of... 'Sebastian would have done anything...he begged me to get him away from his criminal father.'

A criminal father... 18 years ago...

"No." That was not possible. He was a practically an urban myth. "No way Mercer is Michael's dad."

Jamie let out a bitter laugh. "I see you've heard of my ex. Now you're starting to understand."

Michael. The poor guy couldn't catch a break, no matter where he turned. Wait a minute. "Why stay away from Michael? Why kill Sue? Mercer is dead."

Jamie was silent.

No way. I couldn't believe this. If he got away, someone... "You helped him escape."

"Someone inside his circle turned on him. He needed a get-away and I needed him gone before I started to show. And then I had to let my baby go so Mercer had no reason to come back."

"Michael is all alone."

"He had foster families! And as soon as he turned 18, I made sure he came into money."

"You could have met Michael in secret." And not murdered Sue.

"No, I couldn't! You have no idea what it's like when a man as powerful as Mercer considers you his. If he were to come back, Michael and I wouldn't be the only ones to suffer. I did what I did to keep Sheriden safe."

I for one was not a fan of her brand of safety, but I didn't say that.

Jamie looked at me almost sadly. "Your family will be safe."

My family. "But not me."

A saying of the Prophet, something about God giving good people hardship on earth to purify them before death popped into my head. Looking back at the past week, it wasn't likely that was what was happening here. I didn't want to die like this: angry at Abbu, making misery for Ma, not saying goodbye to Adil.

Jamie had been driving to the outer edge of the city, towards the woods.

"I didn't want it to come to this. You're a good kid. Obedient to your parents. Kind to Michael."

Great, my murderer approved of me for her son.

"But after Sylvan told me you went to Sue's a second time, I had to do something."

The old guy… No wonder he found me both times. Jamie had him watching.

"I tried to warn you away."

With a hit and run?

It felt morbid asking, but I was curious. "You framed Nate for Sue's murder."

"I had to," Jamie said. "To take the focus off Michael."

"Who will you pin mine on?"

"You're not going to be murdered," Jamie said. "You're going to run away from your oppressive parents."

I bristled at her description. I knew exactly how flawed my parents were, but she was the last person who should be judging.

"And you're going to become one of the many kids who are never found."

Dread filled me as we approached the edge of the city. It couldn't end like this, with Ma and Abbu never getting any closure. I wouldn't let it.

A cement flower planter made a median in the road just before the back of a sign that welcomed people to Sheriden. I had no idea how Jamie planned to kill me, but I did know I didn't want to be on the dark two-lane road beyond the city limits with her.

I lunged for her gun, hoping the sudden action would scare her into crashing the median. The tussle lasted about two seconds before she flung me off and pointed the gun at me all while swerving the car right to a safe stop onto the paved shoulder.

"I was waiting for that," Jamie said. "You've been surprisingly resilient while helping Michael."

Seeing Jamie turn off the car and unbuckle her belt, I didn't think now was the time to clarify about helping Nate.

"While in another situation I'd appreciate you finding that journal for me, I'm going to have to make sure you stay quiet."

Jamie lifted her gun. In slow motion, I saw the tip aim squarely at my chest. A white light approached. I heard a bang. Felt a crash. And black.

38

When I opened my eyes, I thought I was in a nightmare, turned dream, turned nightmare. Jamie was beside me in the car, bloodied and momentarily disoriented. Past her, through two panes of car windows, was Ma's apoplectic face. Her eyes bulged as she yelled something I couldn't hear. Then Ma opened her door and ran in front of Jamie's car. I watched dazedly until Ma yanked the passenger door open and the night air hit me.

"Why are you sitting there like a *gadha*?" Ma yelled.

Ma was really here. No! I swirled in my seat, my gaze searching Jamie's limp form for the gun. It must have fallen. I reached for the car light but Ma grabbed my arm and wrenched me out of the car. Seeing me plod a couple of steps like the donkey she'd just called me, she rushed to grab my crutches from the back.

"Khushie." Jamie moved slowly, but she was moving, over the centre console and almost out the passenger side. "You should have stayed in the kitchen where you were safe."

I swung my crutch and crashed it over Jamie's head. The reverberations surprised me so much I dropped it.

"Let's go!" Ma dragged me toward our car, but Jamie had fallen back into the car. I could see her arm moving on the floorboards. If she found it she'd shoot through the windshield before we made it away.

"Ma, Jamie has a gun!" I looked from the distance around both cars on one side of us with Jamie in between to the four feet into the woods on the other and made a split-second decision. For once Ma didn't argue and followed me into the woods.

We wound through the trees, me doing my best to keep up, as we tried to gain as much distance between us and Jamie as possible. I put as much pressure as I could on the one crutch I was using, but the uneven ground, darkness, and need to hurry made it impossible to see where I was placing my foot. Tweaks of pain soon became screams that I couldn't ignore. More and more of my weight fell on Ma's petite form. I was too big for her. It was the watermelon/bagel thing all over again.

"Ma." I hissed, pulling to a stop behind a large tree trunk. I lifted my leg to take the weight off my throbbing foot. "We can't get away like this. You have to go."

"Go? And leave my daughter here alone?" Ma's eyes glittered in the darkness. "You will use that *dandee* to keep going. Or I will use it as a *lahtee* to give you the spanking you deserve for putting us in this situation."

Okay. If the choices were using a walking stick over the pain or being whacked until Jamie came to kill us both, I'd keep going. Ma pulled my arm over her shoulders and wrapped an arm around my waist. I bit my lip so hard blood mingled with the fear and adrenaline pumping through me, but I kept going. It felt like we'd been moving forever and not nearly far enough. I wasn't sure how far we'd gone when Jamie's voice paralyzed me.

"That's far enough." Jamie approached from behind with a flashlight and the gun pointed at us.

"Jamie, please." I dropped my arm from Ma's shoulder and stepped forward to cover Ma. "Please don't hurt my mom."

"You know I can't do that, Asiya."

I did know that. I also knew there was no way I could get away. I prayed Ma would realize that too. That for once, she wouldn't be stubborn and just take the cover I was giving her to run.

Ma's forearm knocked the breath out of my lungs as she whacked me back behind her. "You are a coward." Ma told Jamie with all the contempt and disgust she could muster, which was a lot. "What kind of woman shoots a helpless girl?"

"The kind that's protecting her city," Jamie said, adjusting her aim. "And since you're so averse to seeing her die, I'll start with you."

"No!" I lunged for Ma.

The sound of a bullet firing reached me first.

39

Ma!" I searched her frantically. "Ma! Where are you hit? Ma, please be okay!"

"I am not hit." Ma shoved at me. "And you are too *healthee*."

"I…" I scrambled off Ma and turned to where Jamie had been standing. She was wreathing on the ground, her eyes on Constable Keith who approached from behind her with his gun drawn.

"Don't try it." Keith moved to the gun on the ground and kicked it out of Jamie's reach. Dried blood stained the side of his head.

"How did you find us?" I asked Keith once he'd finished putting handcuffs on Jamie and saying police-y stuff into his radio.

"I followed your mother." Keith glared at Ma.

"But how did you find me?" I asked Ma. "I didn't see any

headlights behind us."

"Your Abbu added the data and put the download on your phone while you were at the hospital." She pulled out her phone and showed me a red dot on a map.

They put a GPS tracker on me? I didn't know how I felt about that given the current situation.

"I told you I would watch over you every moment, did I not?" Ma said, angrily. "I did not expect that when I woke up to pray *tahajjud* to thank Allah for keeping my daughter safe, I would find her chasing after danger."

"You should talk." Keith snorted. "I told you to stay back."

"Stay back." Ma muttered. "For who? You? You let that woman hit you over the head! You could not even stop me from going."

Unable to win with Ma, Keith grumbled at me. "I see where you get the stubbornness from."

"If I listened to you, my daughter would be dead!" Ma's anger crumbled into tears.

Keith shifted, glancing around like he was looking for another murderer to deal with rather than Ma's tears.

"Ma, I'm okay." I told her. "You got to me in time."

While I was trying and failing to comfort Ma, more police officers and paramedics arrived.

"Asiya." Jamie called to me from the board they'd strapped her on.

That disposed of Ma's tears instantaneously. She jumped up in Jamie's face. "Do not talk to my daughter, you *shadha goondee*."

Jamie looked past Ma to me. "Protect him for me."

"What did she mean by '*Protect him for me*?'" Keith asked a while later while Ma was giving her statement to a police detective by the side of the road. He seemed to be having a hard time following her braided tale of what happened, what would have happened if not for Allah's mercy, and how I would be spending my life from now on.

"Jamie is Michael's mother." My voice wavered. "With her gone, he has no one."

Keith looked like he was thinking. Even though it was likely a rare occurrence, I didn't want to encourage it in case he thought to ask about Michael's father, so I tried to distract him with "You look gross. You should let the paramedics fix your face."

Keith's eyes narrowed. "I've been wondering. How did Jamie know exactly where I was?"

"Oh. That." My eyes dropped to the ground. "I might have called her… because I thought you were trying to kill me."

"Are you insane?"

"What? You were stalking my house like a creeper!"

"I'd been looking into what you'd said about Nate and things didn't add up. When I heard about your "accident" I knew you pissed off someone more than me with your meddling," Keith said. "I was keeping an eye out and saw a light inside."

"I thought you were the one who framed Nate." I lowered my voice. "Outside the jail, you vowed to come after me. When you didn't come to arrest me, I assumed you… tried to kill me in a hit and run."

"None of that gives me a reason to kill Sue."

"No." I swallowed. "But her letting Sebastian die does."

Keith sucked in a sharp breath. "What do you know about that?"

"I saw his note to her. Who else would have taken it but his big brother?"

Keith's lips tightened. "The note didn't connect him to me."

"Sue's journal did that," I said. "It's in the side door of Jamie's car. The statue she used to club you is in the back seat. And the, uhm, missing appendage from the statue she used to kill Sue is in a tissue paper covered pencil jar on Sue's writing desk."

"You found the phallus." Keith's smirk faded as quickly as it appeared. "Tell me you didn't touch it."

"I wore gloves!"

Keith inhaled a slow breath through his nose. "I could arrest you on so many different charges right now."

"You could." I manoeuvered my crutches back a step. "But do you really want to admit a 17-year-old figured out what you didn't?"

"I would have figured it out much sooner if you hadn't been getting in my way, lying to me from the beginning!"

"I pointed you in the right direction!"

"Let's get a couple of things straight, kid." Keith shoved an unfriendly finger in my face. "First. Before you leave here dreaming up that Jamie had an accomplice, I couldn't have wanted to kill Sue to avenge Sebastian's death because Sebastian's not dead."

Oh.

"He's only dead to me."

Ooh.

"If that troublemaking brat ever has the nerve to cross my path again I'm going to arrest him on the spot." Keith looked like he was anticipating it, with pleasure. "And second, the same goes for you. Get in my way again, and you're taking a first-class trip to juvie."

Ma chose that moment to join us. "Asiya, the police have finished asking questions. We must not stay here any longer. It is night time and we are women alone."

Since I was ever so grateful for it, I didn't point out that she'd left Abbu sleeping and come after me on her own. Anyway, I was happy to cut my conversation with Keith short.

Ma tilted her chin toward him. "Say thank you to Mister Keith,"

Uh, what? I gave Ma a 'you've got to be kidding' look, but she nudged me toward Keith. Who chose this moment to be smugly silent.

Seriously? Now she wanted me to talk to a male?

"By the mercy of Allah, he came in time to stop that *goondee* from shooting us." Ma insisted. "Thank him."

Even though a part of me wanted to whine, 'Why do I have to be the one to do it?' another recognized that Keith had listened about Nate, he'd been at my house looking out for me, and without him… I didn't want to think about how this would have ended without him. "Thank you for saving our lives."

"Just doing my hero thing." Keith shrugged bashfully, while his face lit up like the enabled egomaniac he was. "Now go along home little girl, it's dark outside."

40

My phone rang shrill and way too early the next morning. I'd filled Ma in on the way back in bits and pieces in between her yelling. Abbu had been up by the time we arrived home, so I went through the whole thing, yelling included, again. Daylight was breaking by the time I got to go to sleep.

"ello?"

"Ya-ya!" Em's worried voice assaulted my head. "I heard about the car accident, are you okay?"

I pulled the phone away a bit, and looked down the bed at my foot propped up on pillows. After last night's race through the woods, it was swollen and achy, but I was more than okay. I was alive. "Yeah, I am."

"Oh, that's great," Em said. "Then you can explain to me why the hell you were such a dick to Ali yesterday when he was just trying to help you."

That woke me up. "What are you talking about? Did Firdous or Leyan call you?"

Did everyone leave the lecture yesterday to join me in the main hall of the masjid?

"No, Ali did."

"Come again?" I asked. "I hit my head yesterday. I think I'm hearing things."

"Ali called me, okay! He's a guy who goes to your mosque and he's actually cool. We talk. Get over it already."

Em and Ali were… friends?

"I am not hanging out with him."

"I'm not asking you to," Em said. "But the least you could do is be civil when he's trying to help you out."

"Yeah, well, I could do without his religious advice." Who did he think he was trying to talk to me about Michael when he was all conversant with Em?

"He wasn't trying to give *you* religious advice, Ya-ya," Em said. "He's been trying to tell you that Michael was asking for some."

I sighed. "I already explained to Michael that there was no way we could see each other."

"Maybe he wasn't looking for a way around the rules," Em said. "Maybe Michael wanted to know the rules for himself."

"That's ridiculous," I said. "Why would he want to–"

"You can't think of a single reason why?"

Em was doing her romanticizing thing again. "We're not like that," I said.

"Maybe it's like that for him." Em insisted. "It's possible. And anyway, people have a lot of reasons to want to believe in something bigger and be in a tight community."

I knew how badly Michael wanted to connect deeply with someone or something, and it would just get worse when he heard about his mom, and dad. "Em, I need to talk to Michael."

"Do what you need to do, but we're going to talk about you being nicer to Ali soon."

Not likely.

"Need me to help you sneak out to see Michael?" Em asked.

"Thanks, but I'll figure it out." After everything I'd put my parents through yesterday, I was going to give deception a break.

A little later, I found Abbu getting air in the backyard.

He looked up as I pushed the sliding door closed behind me.

"I know saying sorry doesn't mean anything," I said. "And you have no reason to believe me, but I really do regret putting Ma in danger like that. I..."

"I believe you."

"What?"

"Your Ma told me – through her complaints – that twice you tried to put her life before yours."

"It was my fault she was there. She should never have been at risk."

"And you believe we can live with you risking yours?"

"I... that's not... I didn't mean for any of that to happen."

"What did you think would happen when you went running around trying to clear the man a murderer framed?"

"So, I was supposed to leave Nate to rot in jail?" I asked.

"No one else believed him."

"You should have talked to me, instead of skipping school to call the attention of a killer."

"You say that like you're all reasonable."

Abbu gave me a look.

"Okay fine, *you* are, but then you tell Ma everything and she's not so I get punished for opening my mouth."

"I will not keep secrets from your Ma. If there is something important happening with you, she has the right to know."

"I know," I said sadly. That was our stalemate.

"I won't keep secrets from your Ma." Abbu sighed. "But if you need to talk through an idea with me, something you might want support thinking through, then we can discuss it the two of us."

"And it'll stay between the two of us?"

"So long as it's just an idea, and something I can trust you not to go running off to do on your own, your Ma does not need to know it."

"Okay." It wasn't ideal, but it was a start. "So, I had this idea."

I could see from Abbu's face, he knew where this was going and he didn't like it.

"Jamie was Michael's mom, Abbu. She didn't want to see him and she was a crazy killer." I swallowed, knowing I was asking a lot considering Michael's family, but risked it any way. "He has no one and he's going to be even more alone when he hears this. I really want to be the one to tell him."

Abbu didn't say anything.

I shook my head. "Isn't this what we're supposed to do?

What God's talking about over and over in the Qur'an? Feeding orphans and kindness to the poor? Aren't we supposed to care?"

"So, you care."

"Yes," I said without hesitation. "He's my friend and I don't want him to be all alone. You can be there with me, but please Abbu, let me do this."

I knew I might be shooting myself in the foot, but I had to trust that Michael wouldn't say or do anything to get me in trouble with Abbu.

"What difference does it make who tells him?" Abbu asked.

"Come on, Abbu. Imagine you had no one in the entire world and you were about to receive horrible news. Wouldn't you want to hear it from a familiar face?"

Abbu grappled with that for a moment before looking me directly in the eyes. "Tell me charity is your only intention when it comes to him and I will take you."

I faltered. I couldn't say the words and Abbu knew it.

"It's the only one I'll act on."

"That's not good enough. You are a student. That is your life. You need to focus on school and making a future for yourself," Abbu said. "Not silly feelings that will mean nothing years from now."

"Abbu, please…"

"No." He cut me off. "I won't encourage this."

"You said you'd listen."

"Listening and giving you your way are not the same thing," Abbu said. "I've heard you and my answer is still no."

41

As much as I was dying to find a way to talk to Michael, my last attempt at sneaking out almost got Ma and I killed, so I stayed in my room all weekend. And felt each minute drag by as I wondered what Michael was doing, if he already knew.

A drumroll knock on my door announced Adil.

"Come in."

Adil strolled in with a bowl in his hand and a sympathetic look on his face. "Ma's still really pissed."

"No kidding." I took the bowl filled with massive, Adil-sized scoops of my favourite, peanut butter fudge ripple ice cream.

"Did you really run away with a murderer last night?"

"I didn't mean to."

"And you skipped school all week?"

"Technically I only skipped one and a half times." I sighed.

"And I got caught both times. Actually, I got caught three times," once by Wootten, once by Keith, and once by Wootten and Ma, "while trying to skip once and swing one unnoticed late arrival. That has to be the worst record ever."

"Don't give up, Apa." Adil dropped down next to me on the bed and nudged my shoulder. "You're just not good at it yet."

I hadn't been in the mood to laugh, but Adil managed to make me anyway. "That reminds me, how's your math going?"

"My teacher let me re-write the test and I got a B-." Adil shrugged. "Ma and Abbu are still angry."

"I think a B- is perfectly great."

Adil shrugged and chin-pointed at my melting ice cream. "You're not eating quick enough."

"That's because there's half a tub in this bowl. You know you're going to have to eat this with me."

"Sure, Apa." Adil pulled a second spoon out of the pockets of his shorts. "I got your back."

With Adil's help, the ice cream disappeared quickly. After he left, with nothing better to distract myself, I dived into school work. I worked till I was exhausted enough to sleep.

Monday morning was an ordeal with Ma freaking out about me leaving the house. Since Ma's car was in the garage, Abbu offered to drive me. Ma only relented when we both gave in and let her drive me to school and drop Abbu off at work, so she could pick me up after school too.

I searched for Michael the second I got to school. I didn't find him before first period, but my foot slowed me down in the busy halls. I didn't see him between first and second, and when he wasn't around at lunch I asked everyone who talked to him if they'd seen him. It was like déjà vu. No one had since the week before. I couldn't help but stare at his empty seat during English. *Please God, let him be okay.*

Ma picked me up after school. "I checked with Principal Wootten," she said. "You went to all your classes."

I nodded, unsurprised that tracking me through global positioning wasn't enough for her. After her obsession with keeping me safe had saved my life, the suffocating frustration I usually felt simmered down to mild irritation.

"I have a good news," Ma said, seeming genuinely happy, which was surprising since I was in her presence. "You will be the team leader for the Quizbowl."

I didn't get it. When I walked alone with a boy, Ma was ready to disown me, but when I almost got us both killed, she bounced back and was in reputation recovery mode within a couple days?

"Ma." I fiddled with my seatbelt so I wouldn't have to look at her. "Were you scared at any point in the woods that night?

"What is there to be sacred of? That *goondee*?" Ma's lip curled in disgust. "I knew my Allah would protect me."

I searched for any hint of bravado, but Ma was totally fearless.

"The only thing I need to be afraid of is going to my grave without doing enough good deeds. Starting with raising my children right," Ma said as she parked. "If there is one good thing that has come of it, I think that you have finally learned your lesson."

I totally had. Don't make enemies with Ma, God was

totally on her side.

"When the boy and the girl are alone, Satan is the third," Ma said at the same time. "Now come. I will teach you to cook proper tomato *daal*."

While I sat at the kitchen table chopping tomatoes, the phone rang and Ma picked up. She looked at me, grabbed a towel for me to wipe my hands on and handed me the phone.

"Hello?"

"Asiya." Nate's voice came over the line.

"Um, hi Nate."

"Your mom is standing over you listening, isn't she?"

"Yes."

"Alright, I'll tell you how much I am grateful to you another time," Nate said. "For now, just know if you ever need anything, it's yours."

"You're welcome," I said.

Nate laughed. "Talk to you later."

That night at dinner, everyone else seemed to like the tomato *daal* I'd made with Ma, but I couldn't get myself to get any food down.

Maybe it was Ma's announcement that I'd be volunteering at the *masjid* with Nasreen Aunty that killed my appetite. I didn't even bother arguing. Abbu gave me a weird look, but I went back to swirling grains of rice in streams of *daal*. I was pretty sure he secretly couldn't stand Nasreen Aunty, but wouldn't admit it, nor would he help me get out of it, so what was the point?

Everything went silent and I looked up to see everyone looking at me.

"Sorry, what?"

"How was school today?" Abbu repeated.

I lifted a shoulder. "I got my Chemistry quiz back. I got 92%."

"What happened to the other 8%?" Ma asked immediately.

"A silly mistake," I said. "I'll do better next time."

I waited for Abbu's addition on how important it was to focus on academics, but he shocked me by asking, "Did you talk to Michael?"

"No." I sat up, my wide eyes swinging to Ma. "He wasn't even at school today."

Abbu sighed. "Finish your dinner. I will take you to see him."

"What? Are you trying to ruin your daughter?" Ma asked.

"Khushie, the boy is an orphan," Abbu said.

"We sponsor orphans in Bangladesh."

"This boy is alone in our community."

"He is not our responsibility!"

"When no one takes responsibility, the whole community becomes accountable in front of Allah," Abbu said.

"Then you go!" Ma practically yelled. "Leave Asiya where she will be safe."

"But Ma, I'll be safe," I said, gently. "Abbu will be the third, so Satan can't be."

Ma threw an enraged look my way. "It's still not safe for you."

And by me, she meant my reputation in the community if anyone found out, which I cared nothing about. I just wanted to see Michael.

"We will go quickly," Abbu said gently, but firmly. "Just to see if he is all right."

"I need time to find out where he lives." I told Abbu.

He nodded and went back to eating dinner quietly while Ma alternated between seething quietly and bursting out with angry tirades about how Abbu was ruining me by encouraging this and how I'd connived to make this happen. I finished dinner in record time and called Em. We both harassed everyone who knew Michael until we found someone who knew his address.

Abbu stopped me in the front hall. "You told me yesterday Michael is your friend."

"Yes," I said carefully. "He is my friend."

"I won't have you tell me one thing now and then another when it suits you," he said. "I want you to promise me. Promise me that if I take you to see your friend, he will stay your friend and nothing more."

I paused for a few particularly hard pulse beats, then answered without hesitation. "Let me be his friend through this, and I promise, that's all he will be."

It turned out Michael rented a basement apartment on a quiet street on the opposite side of school from me.

I went along the side of the house with Abbu behind me, took a deep breath, and knocked on his door.

I waited, heart in my throat. I was so starved to see him, just to know that he was okay. I couldn't imagine what he'd be going through if he'd already heard.

I knocked again, louder. Listening impatiently for the sound of his footsteps approaching the door.

"It doesn't look like he is home," Abbu said.

I pounded on his door, refusing to accept that.

A door opened, but not the one I'd been beating on. A woman peered at us from around the front porch.

"If you're here for Michael, you're out of luck," she said. "You and me both."

"What do you mean?" I asked, even though I already knew.

"He took off," she said. "No two months-notice, not even two days-notice. He just packed up his stuff, told me there was nothing for him here, and left."

He was gone.

Michael was the son of a *goonda*, and he didn't even know. I had to find him.

Want more?

Turn the page for a peek at the
Asiya Haque Mysteries, book 2:

MUTAWEENIES

and Other Muslim Girl Problems

Prologue

Sometimes when parents immigrate to a new country they get really concerned with whether their kids are going to keep the culture of their homeland. My parents were really worried that my siblings and I would grow up unable to speak their language.

They figured my older sister and I would learn enough English from Sesame Street. All other activities, including bed time stories had to be in Bangla. For Afiya, that meant when she got to kindergarten she spoke with a slight accent and was put in English as a Second Language for two years before anyone figured out she understood English just fine.

For me it meant growing up with a love of stories that I could only share the awesomeness of in Bangla. Around when I started kindergarten, my favourite was *Ali Baba and the 40 Thieves*. I'd hop around everywhere pointing my finger at things yelling, "Open Sesame!" like I was the coolest secret cave-door opener in town. Except in Bangla, the words for 'Open Sesame!' are 'Cha-ching Fukh!' Which meant that when I got to kindergarten, I was sent to the principal's office and my parents were called in for a disciplinary meeting on my very first day.

I'm in my last year of high school now, and after a bit of trouble at the beginning of the year, I'm completely focused on my future. It's all schoolwork and university applications from here on out. No more getting in trouble for me. Nope. None at all.

Want the latest Asiya Haque info?

For future book releases, excerpts from upcoming books, and fun extras, sign up for the Muslim Girl Problems newsletter at
www.isharadeen.com

Connect with Ishara Deen

Facebook:
www.facebook.com/isharadeen

Twitter:
@isharadeen

Email:
hello@isharadeen.com

If you enjoyed this book, help others who might like it find it too! Tell a friend, share on social media or consider leaving a review on Amazon, Goodreads or anywhere you post reviews.

95364987R00143

Made in the USA
Columbia, SC
09 May 2018